His gaze raked over her as he stood in front of her. Something uncomfortable and unwelcome jittered in her chest as his dark golden gaze met hers.

She wanted to run, but the self-preservation instinct she had so much pride in was no match for the way his gaze pinned her to the spot.

"Al, I presume?" he said, his voice smooth and sounding vaguely...amused. Al didn't have a clue what would be amusing about the situation.

She felt a bit like she'd placed her life into his hands, and she hadn't even spoken.

She gave herself a second to catch her bearings, to focus on the task at hand and not the gold of his eyes. The feeling of being *trapped* and wanting to lean into it. She tried to speak in her usual insouciant low tones, but found her voice much higher than it should be. "Yes, I'm Al."

His beautiful mouth curved, likely at the shake in her tone. "Excellent."

Secrets of the Kalyva Crown

It started with a royal revenge...

Banished following the execution of his parents, Lysias has spent years plotting revenge on the surviving royal of a bloody coup, King Diamandis. Now justice is *finally* within reach, as he has hired someone to pose as the king's long-lost sister...

King Diamandis believed he was the sole surviving member of his royal family. Ruling with an ironclad fist was the only way he knew how to continue their legacy. Until his whole world is tilted on its axis by his supposed sister's royal return...

Soon, both of their carefully constructed plans and lives will be thrown into complete disarray—by love!

Read Lysias and Al's story in
Hired for His Royal Revenge
Available now!

And look for Diamandis and Katarina's story

Coming soon!

Lorraine Hall

HIRED FOR HIS ROYAL REVENGE

**Recycling programs
for this product may
not exist in your area.**

ISBN-13: 978-1-335-73933-9

Hired for His Royal Revenge

Copyright © 2023 by Lorraine Hall

For questions and comments about the quality of this book,
please contact us at CustomerService@Harlequin.com.

Harlequin Enterprises ULC
22 Adelaide St. West, 41st Floor
Toronto, Ontario M5H 4E3, Canada
www.Harlequin.com

Printed in U.S.A.

Lorraine Hall is a part-time hermit and full-time writer. She was born with an old soul and her head in the clouds, which, it turns out, is the perfect combination to spend her days creating thunderous alpha heroes and the fierce, determined heroines who win their hearts. She lives in a potentially haunted house with her soulmate and rambunctious band of hermits-in-training. When she's not writing romance, she's reading it.

Books by Lorraine Hall

Harlequin Presents

The Prince's Royal Wedding Demand

Visit the Author Profile page
at Harlequin.com.

For anyone who ever had a crush on Dimitri.

CHAPTER ONE

AL ASSUMED SHE'D once had a real name and a last name, but she didn't know it. And never would. She had vague memories as a small child of being called Alexandra and being taught how to survive by various people on the streets. Some were kind, some were cruel, some were indifferent, but she had survived.

That was all that mattered most days.

She did not remember anything before being on the streets, so like most of the others she'd met, she assumed her parents were dead or indifferent. Neither mattered. They were gone and she was here.

One of the best methods of survival on the dangerous streets of Athens was to pass herself off as a boy. Even now, at twenty-four, her short stature and small frame meant she could be believed as a teenage boy rather than a grown woman if she dressed and held herself accordingly.

As she did now. She wore tattered baggy pants that hid the shape of her hips. Over her shirts, she wore an oversized coat that gave bulk to her shoulders. Add threadbare boots and shaggy hair pulled back with a small tie, and no one ever questioned her.

She leaned against the corner of a building on a tourist-laden street and surveyed the crowd.

She had a meeting, and she always preferred to meet in the bustling streets for a quick escape should things get *complicated*. Trading in information had a tendency to have tempers flaring, particularly in those men who fancied themselves powerful...then threw tantrums like children when they did not get their way...or could not hide their misdeeds.

Al usually didn't take jobs from people she hadn't been referred to and hadn't checked out carefully. She tended to be very careful about people who approached *her*. She made sure she knew everything about a *client* before she even spoke to them. But this particular afternoon, she didn't *truly* know who she was meeting. Only that the payout she had been promised was far too much to resist.

It was enough to possibly get her out of the spy game forever. In the beginning, it had been exciting. To realize that, since no one paid much attention to a little beggar on the street, she could hear things and see things that other people found useful.

And would pay for.

But as she'd gone from offering up information she *happened* to witness or overhear to people coming to her *for* information, spying had gotten more complicated, more dangerous. Like today.

It was possible this whole meeting was a trap. Things were getting a little…hot. She'd uncovered the misdeeds of a few too many powerful men who were now on the lookout for a boy spy roaming the streets of Athens. Who wanted Al dead.

She could shake that identity, of course. Live life as she truly was: a young woman. She could find a new city to live in as a boy. But those options seemed just as dangerous as the men after her.

At least they were the enemy she *knew.*

Her life had been the streets and survival for as long as she could remember, but she was tired of subterfuge and lies and mystery and danger. She wanted something…pleasant. Relaxing.

Safe, most of all.

This payout could buy her all of that. She only had to bend a few of her rules to get it and hope the mysterious man who'd sent his men to approach her was on the up-and-up.

So she waited for a man. That was all she knew about her client. His employee—a taciturn mountain of a man—had told her to stand exactly here and wait for his boss to approach.

She watched the crowd carefully. A few people looked her way, usually nervously. Women clutching their purses a little tighter, especially if Al arranged her face to look particularly surly. But most people just looked right past her short frame and out-of-the-way stance, more focused on their daily routines or the sights they wished to see.

Al did not see much point staring at ruins, vestiges of a life so long ago no one alive today would even recognize it. She much preferred watching the living people. How they reacted, what they did, the words they spoke in a variety of languages as they passed.

She was beginning to grow antsy as the agreed-upon time came and went. Frowning, she scanned the crowd around her one more time. That was when she caught the glimpse of a tall man in white. He seemed to cut through the crowd like some kind of archangel. Or apparition. Or just a deadly sweep of a sword.

People moved out of his way—some without seeming to realize it, some watching him move in awe. He did not ask anyone to. He did not excuse himself. It was just…done.

He was stunning—it was the only word she could think of. Like some gladiator brought to life, polished up perhaps for a portrait, because even though he looked like he could *handle* a fight, his expensive suit and bright white clothes didn't suggest he'd seen one recently. His dark hair was swept back, his face sculpted and bronzed as if perfectly created to draw attention to his eyes. Sharp, gold. *Obviously* dangerous.

And he was walking straight for her.

Al ordered herself to maintain her lazy posture, her combative expression, but it was more and more difficult to hold the closer he got. He walked right up to her, practically towering above her so that he blocked out the sun in the little alcove she'd agreed to meet him in.

Because this had to be the *him* who wanted to meet her—well, Al. She hadn't been given a name when his employee had talked to her, but she knew who he was now. It was nearly impossible to spend any time in Athens and not know *his* face.

Lysias Balaskas. *Billionaire.* Self-made, at that. One of those stories people trotted out to prove *anyone* could achieve *anything*, because Lysias himself had, allegedly, been a product of the streets. According to the people who spoke of it, Lysias had gotten himself a job above his station as a young man and then worked his way up until he'd owned…just about everything there was to own. People said it was because he was brilliant and charming and determined and hardworking.

Al knew that success, especially success of Lysias's magnitude, required all those things but also a great deal of luck. Or *she* would be CEO of some conglomeration of companies that did something with… something. Because she could be all those things, if given the chance.

She had decidedly not been given the chance.

His gaze raked over her as he stood in front of her. He took her all in with a considering way that had her wanting to sink deeper into her baggy clothes and disappear into the shadows, because the hairs on the back of her neck stood on end. Something uncomfortable and unwelcome jittered in her chest as his dark golden gaze met hers.

She wanted to run, but the self-preservation instinct she had so much pride in was no match for the way his gaze pinned her to the spot.

"Al, I presume?" he said, his voice smooth and sounding vaguely…amused, when Al didn't have the first clue what would be amusing about the situation.

She felt a bit like she'd placed her life into his hands, and she hadn't even spoken.

She gave herself a second to get her bearings, to focus on the task at hand and not the gold of his eyes. The feeling of being *trapped* and wanting to lean into it. She tried to speak in her usual insouciant low tones but found her voice much higher than it should be. "Yes, I'm Al."

His beautiful mouth curved, likely at the shake in her tone. "Excellent."

Lysias Balaskas found himself wholly and uncharacteristically uncertain about this *Al*. Though he had heard nothing but positives about the boy and his ability to find even the most hidden information, something about the way he stared made Lysias feel even more aware than he usually was.

As a man bent on revenge, he was *always* aware. Of who looked at him. Of what people thought. Of where he was and how he moved. Because unlike most people who walked these streets, Lysias had only one goal in his life.

And he allowed *no* distractions.

"Why don't we take a bit of a walk, my boy," Lysias offered in an effort to perhaps jolt the boy into finding his wits about him.

Lysias tended to have this effect on people. He knew he was good-looking—add money and power, and people often found themselves at a loss for words. It was just an everyday occurrence for him. Though he'd expected perhaps *more* of the boy he'd heard had uncovered the secrets of some of the most powerful and dangerous men in Greece.

"You have a job for me," this Al said, taking a step next to him. Lysias noted the way the boy's eyes surveyed the crowd. Calm, cool, assessing. Looking for danger.

Well, that was more like it. Clearly he'd sussed out who Lysias was and, maybe after his initial surprise, would now behave the canny spy Lysias had been promised.

"There is a very old rumor I would like you to look into for me," he said, walking through the crowd as though he had not a care in the world. But his attention was on Al—the way the boy moved, what he looked at and how he reacted to everything Lysias had to say. "It involves the kingdom of Kalyva."

There was no flicker of surprise or reaction. Only a shrug. "I do not know this place."

"It is a small island. Tiny really. They are very independent, very private. And ruled by a king." And Lysias wanted to destroy said king, with his bare hands. But since that was not an option, he would settle for subterfuge to get his revenge. To enact all the destruction King Diamandis deserved.

"And what do you want with it?"

"That is not your concern. Your concern is to find out everything you can on the murder of Princess Zandra Agonas on Kalyva twenty years ago."

"You want me to get you information on some old murder that happened on an island I've never even heard of?" Al asked suspiciously. He looked up, but the minute their gazes met, the boy looked back down. "Seems a stretch."

"The entire royal family was murdered in a bloody coup. Except the current king. The rumor is Princess Zandra's body was the only one not recovered," Lysias said, unconcerned by Al's skepticism. "I need to know that this is true beyond a doubt. It will require you to find a way to get close enough to King Diamandis to discover the absolute truth, or what he believes to be the truth anyway. I will cover any costs on top of the already generous payout my man discussed with you."

The boy's mouth turned down, and there was just…something off about him. Lysias felt that old itch between his shoulder blades. A telltale sign that something was amiss.

But he had been assured of this boy's skill and, having once been a boy on these streets himself, knew what a smart one could do with an opportunity.

Besides, Lysias would make sure he had the upper hand.

He always did.

So he would continue forward. His revenge on King Diamandis had been twenty years in the making, and no matter what Al found or didn't, Lysias would never give up.

The king was the reason his parents had been killed, the reason Lysias had scrabbled on the streets for the remainder of his childhood after being exiled from Kalyva.

The king would pay. For everything.

"You will travel to Kalyva with one of my men. Tonight. Then you will set about finding what the king knows. You will report to Michalis, who will, in turn, report to me. No one can know about our connection once you're on Kalyva. Trust me when I say that it would be as bad for you as it would for me."

The boy pursed his lips and kept walking. He glanced behind them once, so Lysias did the same, wondering what the boy was worried about. A tail? The police?

"Travel costs extra," he said at last.

"Was my initial offer not generous enough?"

Al stopped, stepping out of the way of teeming tourists with ease. He glowered up at Lysias, or tried to. "It's not generosity—it's compensation. Besides, I know how much you're worth."

"You know how much people *think* I'm worth."

He grinned at the boy. "The truth is beyond most people's comprehension."

The boy's eyes widened, and his cheeks turned oddly pink before he looked away once more. He studied the world around them, clearly considering the deal. "I want some money up front."

"So you can run?"

He shrugged. "Call it insurance."

Al tried to keep walking, but Lysias reached out and took him by the arm. He pulled the boy close enough, all the way onto his toes, to get his point across. Not a violent threat. Lysias no longer *needed* violence. *He* was threat enough.

"Know this, boy. I *will* track you down if you take my money and run. To the ends of the earth. No one crosses me. I simply do not allow it."

Wide, dark eyes watched him. The boy was slight, with delicate features. Lysias couldn't fathom how he'd survived this long on the streets, let alone doing what he did. Part of Lysias's defense as an adolescent had been his size and strength. His ability to fight his way out of any predicament.

Al clearly would not be able to do that.

The boy jerked his arm away and Lysias let him, but something about the interaction left him…suspicious. He couldn't put his finger on what struck him as *off* about the boy, but he didn't trust him.

"I want an up-front payment," Al insisted. He nodded to the watch on Lysias's wrist. "That'll do."

Lysias raised an eyebrow. "Do you have any idea what this watch is worth?"

Al grinned, cocky and amused, the first glimpse at a boy who would make a very good spy. "Oh, I've got a pretty good idea, *ploúsios*."

Lysias was surprised to find himself enjoying the boy's cheek. Much better than the odd stares that left him feeling as if something were all wrong here.

Lysias slid the watch off his wrist and dropped it into Al's hand. "It would be easy to track that down if you defy me."

"Yes," Al agreed. Simply. Easily. He pocketed the watch, surveyed the crowds around him once more. "When and where?"

"Midnight. My private marina. I'm assuming you can find this on your own."

"Naturally."

"I'll be there with my man of affairs, so you can be assured you are meeting the correct person. I will ensure you are on the boat and on your way to Kalyva. Michalis will cover your costs while on the island and be your main point of contact. If you do not find me the information I require in a week, we'll reevaluate the deal."

Al didn't study him. He studied his own feet. Then he shrugged. "All right." And without a handshake or anything else, he took off on a run. Quickly disappearing into the crowd.

Lysias watched. He didn't think the boy was bolting from *him*. His impression of the boy was someone capable and likely to show up tonight and do the work on Kalyva, but *something* was off. Wrong.

Lysias knew this in his bones.

So, after the boy disappeared into the crowd, Lysias followed.

CHAPTER TWO

AL TOOK OFF for a few reasons. Number one, she knew she was being watched—and not by the magnetic Lysias—though him too. No, someone out in that crowd wanted to hurt her. She'd noticed the same man in too many places today, and while she'd never caught his eyes on *her*, it was too much of a coincidence.

She had to lose him. So she ran.

But it wasn't the *only* or most alarming reason she'd felt compelled to run. Lysias Balaskas was… problematic. She couldn't seem to hold his gaze without blushing. She was far too interested in the quirk of his beautiful mouth than what it said.

And those *eyes*. Nothing in her short but eventful life had prepared her for the effect this man had on her. She had dealt with the wealthy, the powerful, the good-looking, but he was in a category all his own. Deep within and elemental, Lysias was different. It terrified her.

Worse, it enticed her.

She had to get away from him. So she'd bolted. With his watch, sure, but that didn't mean she *had* to take his deal. If she decided not to meet him at his marina, she'd return it to him without him knowing it and stand him up tonight.

She pulled a face as she dove right into crowds, then swiveled out again. The marina, a boat with a stranger. She didn't like the idea of traveling with anyone, let alone Lysias's employee. Just her and some *stranger* in the middle of the sea. Not even the unnerving man she'd met this afternoon—not that she trusted *him* either.

Al trusted no one.

She skittered down a tight alley, the hot sun beating down on her. She had a lead on her pursuer, but she could still *feel* that shadowy figure following her—she knew too well what pursuit felt like. She hadn't lost them yet.

Maybe a new location would be good. She had never heard of this island. Maybe it was because she was uneducated and unworldly, but maybe other people didn't know about it either. It might be the perfect opportunity to escape everything breathing down her neck here in Athens on someone else's dime.

She ducked down a wider alley, crossed a busy street, always keeping an eye behind her. She'd been the quarry in a few of these little chases, and she didn't revel in it, but she knew how to escape.

Had to escape.

An island would be an escape, wouldn't it? Strangers were dangerous, but the devil she knew was getting a little too close. A little too scary.

Maybe it was time for a new devil. Lysias definitely fit the bill.

Kings and murdered princesses worried her, but she'd been slipping in and out of the affairs of the rich and powerful for years now. Were royalty all that different? A change of scenery, a payout that would allow her to be herself, not Al…

It could all work out.

If she escaped her current mess. She climbed a ladder up onto someone's balcony, then took a hop over to the next and the next. Once she got to the other edge of the building, she jumped off, startling a young couple sharing a dessert on a bench. She flashed them a boyish grin, then darted across the street, holding her hat on her head as she did so.

And still someone chased her. Getting closer. Panic began to clog her lungs, but that was certain death. She had to think clearly, rationally. She was certain she was doing just that, but then she tripped over a man's foot, and though she narrowly missed a fall, a group of men angrily shouted at her.

It startled her, rattled her as much as the meeting with Lysias had, and so she ran without fully taking into account where she was.

A fatal mistake, as she ran right into an alley with no exit. She studied the wall in front of her, looking for any sort of foothold. Some way to climb it. Some way out.

There was nowhere to run. She blew out a breath as her world crashed around her.

She supposed she should take her fate philosophically. She would die at the hands of someone else. It had always been possible. And she'd done some good with her insignificant life. Uncovered many a man's misdeeds.

It was a shame she'd never truly gotten to live as herself. Have some sort of *life*. For some reason, that made her think of Lysias and his golden eyes and wicked smile. Which was foolish enough she turned to face her attacker.

He had a long knife. A scar that ran from his temple to where it disappeared under the collar of his shirt.

"That looks bad," she said, jutting her chin at the scar. "I suppose you're going to do the same to me?" She eyed the knife and tried to breathe through the terror. Hold on to bravado. But she'd always had a fear of blades, more so than even a gun. A gun could take you out quick.

A knife took its time. A knife was torture.

Her legs shook, but she told herself to fight her way out. She'd get hurt. Stabbed, sure, and that was a nightmare of hers, but if she just *ran*, she could stay alive. Maybe. If she didn't bleed to death. If he didn't fully overpower her.

So she went with that. She just ran. Plowed right into the man, hoping to dislodge the knife. She didn't, but she *did* surprise him so that he fell back.

Of course, that had her tripping over *his* body. But she got passed him.

She scrambled to get to her feet, could see the daylight and the alley opening and all the freedom it represented. But the moment she was *almost* there, the man's hand caught her around the ankle and jerked, sending her sprawling on the hot, hard ground. She fought desperately, but she was no match for the man who crawled on top of her.

She clawed, she kicked, but nothing dislodged him from his purpose. He used the knife to roughly cut away her shirt, and panic beat so hard in her chest she couldn't breathe. She saw the dawning realization on his face, even as she bucked and fought and kicked harder with panic, dread, the desperate desire to survive.

"You're a woman. A shame we couldn't have some fun, but my orders are clear. Consider this a gift from Mr. Pangali," he said, mentioning one of the powerful men she'd uncovered as a liar and a cheat *and* a murderer.

Slowly—as if he enjoyed causing pain—her attacker began to press the sharp edge of the knife through the bonds that held her breasts down and then upward—not just cutting away the fabric but slicing into her skin. Trying to create the long, jagged line from chest to temple that he had.

Pain had an unholy noise escaping her throat, and she bucked with all of her strength. Much to her surprise, the knifeman flew off her. He let out a yelp of pain as he crashed hard against the wall of the building.

Now able to see the entire alley, Al realized she had not magically overpowered her attacker.

Lysias was here.

For a moment, she was frozen. He'd *saved* her. She sucked in a breath, but everything hurt. Pain radiated from her chest, and the sticky warm feeling of blood seeping out of the knife wound made her dizzy.

She had to get up…she had to…

Lysias leaned over her, those golden eyes holding her still—but only for a moment. Because he reached out for the torn piece of shirt. "Where are you hurt?"

She pushed him away, tried to scoot out from his grasp, his gaze.

"Stop fighting, boy," he said impatiently. "I'm going to help you," he said so disgustedly, so authoritatively, she hesitated.

And in that hesitation, all was lost. Because his hands were on her where she bled, and all she tried to hide from the world was clear to him. She knew it when his hand rested over her breast—bound but not enough now that she'd been *stabbed* there.

He pulled back, looked at his bloody hand, then down at her. "You're not a boy."

She scurried out from under him, using his surprise as a means of escape. But there was nowhere to go. He blocked the only exit. So she stood, breathing ragged, the blood trailing down her chest and too much of her exposed. Who she truly was, *exposed*.

But she wouldn't cower. He'd saved her from one threat, but that didn't mean he wasn't one himself. She had to keep fighting.

"You're not even a girl," he said, studying her critically. "You're a woman."

Lysias did not often find himself shocked. In fact, he could not remember the last time someone had pulled such a con over on him.

Of course, he'd *known* something was off about the boy, but he had not considered Al might be a *woman*.

She tilted her chin upward, all challenge. She did not speak. Those dark eyes looked at him with pure hate. But pain also swirled in their dark depths.

He had already instructed his guard to take care of the assailant, so it was only he and Al—the *woman*—standing in this dingy alley in a poor, dangerous neighborhood of Athens.

He circled her, but she moved as well, never allowing him to be at her back. Smart woman.

She had survived on the streets for some time, he supposed, pretending to be a boy, though she'd narrowly escaped a gruesome end here. Intriguing.

But before he could work through all this and what it might mean, she needed medical attention. "Come," he said, holding a hand out to her to encourage her obedience.

She did not take it. She clutched her torn shirt together and studied his hand as suspiciously as if he were holding the knife. "Where?"

"Somewhere we can clean you up."

"I can take care of myself," she said.

"And yet, here you are. In an alley. Stabbed and bloody and saved. By me, I might add." The blood trailing down her golden skin and dirty shirt was concerning enough, but her face was also dangerously pale, and she reached out to stabilize herself against the wall.

Which made his decision for him. She had been manhandled enough, but she needed a doctor. He marched forward, did his best to avoid hurting her and carefully scooped her off her feet, despite her protests.

She fought initially, but the hiss of pain seemed to force her to realize her predicament. So she stilled here in his arms. Tiny thing that she was.

His thoughts were dark as he marched her to his car. That desperate men with knives and cruel men with power would try to harm someone in such a lower position than they.

"What happened to…him?" she asked, as they approached his waiting car. His driver stood expressionless, back door open and ready.

"My guard has taken care of it. Your attacker will be dispatched to the nearest police station."

"Without a victim, nothing will happen to him," she said, devoid of any emotion. "Even with a victim, really. It hardly matters anyway. He's just paid muscle."

He knew from experience living on the streets tended to beat the belief in justice out of a person. But he would ensure her attacker found justice—as well as the man who'd sent him.

He had built himself up out of the depths of poverty and abandonment to be the hand of justice himself.

"I'll make sure he pays."

She looked up at him. Her eyes were dark, that earnest gaze she hadn't been able to hold before. Maybe she could now because they were hazed with pain and worry. *Fear.* And because he knew her secret.

He did not relish frightening any woman, but it frustrated him that she would fear when he had just *saved* her. "A thank-you wouldn't go amiss."

She said nothing.

He found his mouth wanting to scowl, but he would not allow such feelings. He had saved her. She *would* thank him eventually. And he would get what he needed out of her.

This did not change their deal.

"Now, watch your head," he said, surprised at the softness in his tone. Uncomfortable with it. But she was injured. And a *woman*.

He crouched to carefully deposit her on the seat, then skirted the car to the other side. He slid into the seat next to her. He had already instructed his driver to take them to his private home outside the city center.

He had many residences in and around Athens, many closer, but this was the one he went to when he wanted privacy rather than attention. Though her wound needed a doctor, keeping her identity on the down-low was just as important. For her. And for him—as he had plans for this woman.

Old plans, and now new plans as well.

He reached forward and pulled open one of the many compartments in the back of his car. Though he tended to stay out of physical fights these days, he was a street urchin himself at heart. He had a first aid kit and, even more importantly, a nice bottle of brandy.

He handed her some gauze. "Hold that over where you're bleeding. Wouldn't want you soiling my seats." Then he poured her a small amount of brandy in a glass and handed it to her.

She took the gauze, but shook her head vehemently at the alcohol. He shrugged, took the drink himself, enjoying the slow burn of the expensive liquor. He wished it would settle the dark feeling coiled tight within him. Though he was familiar with such feeling, it rarely expanded any farther than the object of his revenge.

He made a few calls to prepare his residence. For a visitor. For someone who needed medical attention. She watched him the entire time, pushed up against the door as if she might try to escape the minute the car stopped. As if *he* were her attacker.

So he stayed on his side of the seat and watched her right back. Considering. Because this unexpected turn of events might actually be quite…good. For him, of course, but he was a fair man, mostly. He'd make it good for her as well.

She had her back straight, but she was clearly holding herself gingerly due to the pain. She clutched her torn shirt together, pressing the gauze to it. Without her hat, with her hair untied, she looked a bit more feminine, but really she could have kept the pretense if her attacker hadn't cut through the bonds that flattened her chest.

"What is your name?" he asked, finding himself unduly curious.

"Al."

"That is a boy's name."

She shrugged and offered nothing more.

"Do you dress as a boy because you wish to? Or as a disguise?" She could be pretty, he supposed, given the right amenities and opportunities. Which suited the new plan he was formulating.

"Life on the streets is easier for a boy."

"Not easy." He had learned that at the age of twelve. When he had been tossed out of Kalyva with *nothing*. By the king, who'd barely been older than himself.

"No, but easier," she replied. She shifted in her seat, clearly trying to cover a wince. "Once you pay me, I will live as I please," she said haughtily. But he knew enough about desperation, about wishing for better, to hear the yearning in her tone.

And the fact her little dream was missing an important step in getting paid. "Once you complete your job, and *then* I pay you, will you live as a woman?"

She hesitated. "I don't see what it matters to *you*, but yes. As long as it's safe to."

"And what will you call yourself then?"

She hesitated, as if considering the ramifications of him having such a small piece of information. "Alexandra, I suppose. Though I've gone by Al so long I don't know why I'd change." She turned to look out the window, though it was tinted, so not much could be made out. "Where are you taking me?"

"My private residence. A medical professional will check you out—one I pay to be discreet. Once we know the extent of your injuries, we will determine the next course of action." But he already had the plan. A way to move up his timelines.

A way to taste revenge before the month was out.

Because revenge was his only goal. Not understanding this street urchin, no matter how interesting she might be. She was simply a tool to get what he wanted—a tool he would compensate generously for her work.

He studied the woman critically. She had the right coloring, more or less, when she wasn't pale from an attack. What didn't quite fit with her hair, with her nose and mouth, could easily be fixed in a salon or with the right clothes and makeup.

"I'm fine," Al said stupidly, in his opinion. "I just need a bandage or something. Take me back to *my* home. I'll find out about the princess. This won't stop me."

Lysias made no move to entertain her little attempt at orders. *He* did not get ordered around. "Do you *have* a home?" he asked instead.

"Perhaps not as fine as yours, but certainly a place to lay my head."

Yes, she was going to fit into his plan very, very nicely. The obstinate lift of her chin, the challenge in her eyes. With the right training, that could be seen as royal. "I'm afraid our plans have changed."

She got that wild look, panic, through and through. Like when she'd bolted from him in the crowd. "I don't want them to."

"Alas, I find that you now have two uses for me." He smiled at her, quite pleased with this turn of events. He understood that part of his success came from his tenacity, his spite that drove him in everything he'd done since the age of twelve, but there was also the element of luck to how far he'd been able to climb.

And luck was once again on his side.

"Asteri mou," he said, smiling at her. "It is your lucky day after all. You are to become my bride."

CHAPTER THREE

AL WAS CERTAIN she must have heard wrong. He must speak a different language—one where *bride* meant something else entirely.

"We will likely be able to avoid an *actual* union, of course," Lysias continued as if this were normal. As if…

Maybe she had a head injury. Surely she did since she was riding in this luxurious car, a stab wound on her chest, going to who knew where without having put up much of a fight. It was his eyes. His authoritative way of speaking that didn't feel like commands so much as the only reasonable course of action. It was the blood loss, the trauma. It was everything except *reasonable*, *rational* and *sane*.

"But, should push come to shove, you will be compensated for this as well. A large payout is your goal, is it not?"

"Money, not a husband." Bride. Husband. She pressed her free hand to her forehead. Was she in some sort of fevered delusion?

"Even a billionaire for a husband?" Lysias replied, though she didn't believe his feigned surprise for a second. Though he had stepped in to save her, though he was being hands off and allegedly going to get her medical attention, she saw that he was not really different from the man who'd sent her attacker.

Lysias had decided something—regardless of how strange—and thought he could sit there and smile charmingly and she would just go along. That she wouldn't poke or argue or *uncover* all that he was.

"*Especially* that," she said, giving an injured little sniff. "I have no interest in men of wealth and power who think of little else."

"It is not my wealth and power that consumes me, *Alexandra*. Though they are impressive."

He practically *purred* the name, which wasn't hers, but it seemed almost as if him speaking it into existence made it so. And every syllable felt like a caress down her spine. Not just a jitter in her chest but something dangerous and yearning blooming deep within her. Stuck again in the direct beam of his golden gaze.

Al tried to breathe normally, to let out all that had gotten clogged without giving away how affected she was by…him. But it was no use. His smile deepened.

She scowled at him. "Then what does *consume* you?" she asked, being sure to imbue the word "consume" with as much disdain as possible even though pain and fear coursed through her.

"Revenge," he said. Simply. Bland, almost, but

she saw the fierceness in his gaze, in the way he held himself. "I was wronged many years ago. And I will not rest until that wrong has been righted."

Every word got more intense. Deeper and darker. She realized in the brief flash of it, there then gone, that he kept this fury banked or hidden away under some kind of mask. But it was there. Perhaps *always*.

And she did believe that it did in fact drive him. That he was a dangerous man, but she had never been afraid of dangerous men. Fear never accomplished anything good, so she had done all she could to eradicate it.

"Maybe I don't wish to help you enact revenge," she said.

He did not respond with surprise or fury as she had expected. Maybe even hoped. Both reactions she would understand.

The cold, cutting smile was not one she could make sense of.

"Let me tell you a little story about the kingdom of Kalyva." He leaned forward, those gold eyes seeming to gleam here in the dim back seat, where even the daylight couldn't make it through the tinted windows. And those eyes acted like some sort of hypnotist's tool to keep a woman still and rapt with whatever he said.

"It is small and independent, as I said. Some would call it backward, old-fashioned. They would not be wrong. The king and queen of my youth were good people, or so it seemed, but they were not *strong*.

And so, as dissatisfaction with the old ways mounted, they buried their heads in the sand and ignored all the whispers, all the signs. And though the bloody coup ended their lives and the lives of all but their oldest child, the kingdom remained, because the eldest child survived."

Al didn't realize she'd leaned forward, that she held her breath, waiting for the rest of the story.

"The new king was not much older than a boy, but he was full of revenge. Understandably. But his revenge blinded him, and he had no interest in who was actually innocent or guilty. He was only interested in causing his own brand of bloodshed. He sentenced my *innocent* parents to death, labeled me a traitor, claiming I had not raised the necessary concerns against my parents' plot against the princess, and had me sent to Athens. With nothing. I was *twelve*."

Lysias was cold, angry, and even his hand had curled into a fist. Perhaps she should be afraid of him. He was a large man. A strong man—he'd thrown her attacker off as if it were nothing. He was full of fury and revenge.

But all she could think of was a boy of twelve tossed from everything he knew. Lost. She had always been lost, but she had no idea what had existed before. It would be much harder to adapt at twelve.

It was impossible to picture him as a youth, and yet she felt for the boy he must have been all the same.

"You are an avenger, Alexandra," he said, though

she thought she preferred Al to the overly feminine name she'd considered going by someday and foolishly told him about. "You have sought, at your own peril, to unmask the misdeeds of many a powerful man."

He was right, but it felt like losing whatever little power she had here to admit that. So she lifted a shoulder, though it hurt—both her wound and her conscience. "For a price."

Lysias leaned back, some of that controlled anger banked in his eyes. He smiled at her. "Yes, a price. A smart person always takes payment for the work they do. But the payment doesn't matter if you're dead, and you have risked death. You've decided to take that risk, again and again, because you wished to see justice done, regardless of what you might lose."

She did not know how to argue with that. It was only the facts. Though she took the money to survive and had gotten into the whole spying on people game as a means of survival, she had taken increasingly higher profile people down. At her own risk, because she'd wanted to see powerful men who did bad things *fall*. Because she had, too often on the streets, seen the victims of their abuses of power.

Lysias's smile widened when she said nothing. It was as if he could see through her, down to her very soul. Which had that same foreign warmth from earlier bloom deep within her. Her instinct was to look away, but his eyes compelled her.

"So now, Alexandra, you will help me enact my justice. Once and for all."

Lysias watched the emotions play out over Alexandra's face. He would turn her into Alexandra even though she tried very hard to keep her mask in place, a boyish kind of challenge she must have perfected over the years.

But she was hurt, and he knew his story compelled her. He could see it in the way she looked at him now: less hate, less suspicion, though some of both still. But it was all softer, there in her dark eyes.

"We are not that different, you and I," he told her. "We come from a similar place. Once my plan is a success, you can have much of this too." He gestured to the luxurious car they were in.

"Much, but not all?" she replied.

"No one can have it all. Except me."

She did not smile in return, but something lightened in her gaze that made him want to *genuinely* smile, instead of the media smile he trotted out to play the role of Lysias Balaskas. A man *not* bent on revenge.

The car slowed, no doubt pulling through the gates to his expansive estate. "Ah, we are home. We will get you patched up, then discuss the plan."

"And if I refuse to help you?" she asked.

He studied her. This woman, who'd posed as a boy for so long. Bloody in the back of his car. Alive because he'd saved her. And she dared suggest refusal? It should be an insult. An outrage.

He had no idea why he wanted to *laugh*. He did *not*, but he wanted to. He kept his gaze on her, his expression carefully bland. Because Lysias Balaskas had built himself into a man who got *whatever* he wanted.

And he would have his revenge.

"Your refusal is immaterial. You will do everything I say. For this, you will be rewarded. Beyond your imagination. This I promise you. But there will be no *refusal*. I have saved you. I know your secret. You are mine for the foreseeable future."

Her outrage was a thing of beauty. No matter how disheveled and bedraggled she was, her eyes flashed. Temper brought some much-needed color to her cheeks. She *could* be beautiful.

She *would* be once he was done with her.

"I have never cowed to a man before, *Lysias*," she said, drawing his name out like one might draw out a curse.

He found himself aroused by it. *Interesting*, but not something to think too much on in the current moment.

The car had stopped, and the woman needed medical attention for certain. The driver opened his door first. So Lysias got out without response. The doctor he kept on his payroll to ensure any and all necessary silence stood at the entrance.

Lysias waved him over, and the man was quick to

approach the car. Lysias himself opened the door to Al's seat. She looked up at both of them with mulish distrust.

"Let me have a look now," the doctor said briskly.

She looked at the doctor, then at Lysias, then back. Then, as if sensing she couldn't really do *anything* until someone attended that wound, she dropped the gauze for the doctor.

Lysias left them to it. Seeing the wound on her created too many conflicting feelings. He only had room in his life for one revenge. Though he made a quick call to his guard to check on the fate of the attacker and then made a few more calls to ensure the man never saw light outside of a cell again.

He also set in motion a clandestine investigation that would put whoever was behind the attack behind bars. He considered Al—*Alexandra*—under his protection now, until his revenge was seen through. That protection included justice.

His staff would ensure she did not escape, and he had much work to do to move up the timeline of his plans. So he went to work.

A few hours later, he was summoned to dinner by his housekeeper. "And our houseguest?" he asked.

"She has been seen to by the doctor. Stitched up and cleaned up. We suggested she rest and eat in her room, but she insisted on seeing you, so we've seated her at the table should you wish to dine together."

"Excellent."

Lysias walked through his home, realizing with a

start the odd feeling in his chest was excitement. But of course he was excited. His plans for revenge were within his grasp, truly, for the first time.

He strode into his dining room, a finely appointed formal affair he usually entertained businessmen and diplomats and other influential people at.

Now there was a young woman with light brown hair at his table and he stopped short. She wore a shapeless but comfortable-looking cotton dress one of his staff must have obtained for her. Her face was fresh and she wore no makeup. Her hair was pulled back, much as it had been when she'd been posing as a boy, but it had been brushed rather than left shaggy and unwashed.

She looked like a stranger. A female stranger.

Until she met his gaze with that haughty disdain she'd tried so hard to maintain in the car. *That* he recognized.

"This is a lot of work just to eat," she said by way of greeting. "Is this what happens when you have so much money you don't know what to do with it? You have to make simple things into a wasteful production?"

"Perhaps I simply love a production, wasteful or otherwise." He studied her as he took the seat across from her. Her color was much better, and she didn't hold herself as though she were in pain. "How are you feeling?" he asked as the staff brought out dinner.

Al watched the food with avid interest. "That doctor, if he really is a doctor, stitched me up. Gave me something for the pain. I'm not supposed to lift anything heavy or go scaling buildings and facing off with men with knives for a few days, but somehow, I will survive."

Her bland description of events amused him. But not enough to remember the one thing he hadn't gotten from her. "I'm still waiting for that thank-you."

She grabbed the fork and the knife on either side of her plate and merely scowled at him before attacking the food angrily. She did not thank him or say anything else.

But he was a patient man. When he wanted to be. He sipped his wine and watched her. She certainly still *moved* like a young, wild boy. "How many times did you try to escape?"

She hesitated before lifting the next bite to her mouth, decidedly not answering his question.

"My staff will inform me, so you might as well say."

"Twice." She stabbed a piece of meat with her fork. "You kidnapping me doesn't make me too keen on helping you with this whole revenge plot. Taking down a powerful king or no. Payout or no."

"I saved your life. Brought you to a doctor. I am feeding and clothing you. This is hardly a kidnapping."

"It's not *not* a kidnapping," she grumbled, gulping from her glass. Though he had spent years on the streets, he *had* been raised in a palace. As the help's child, yes, but he had learned how to handle himself at a dinner even before he'd become wealthy, thanks to a friendship with the young royals.

"Table manners," he muttered. "You have much to learn." Much work to do if he wanted to leave in a few days. Because for many years, he'd wished to return to Kalyva with a fake Princess Zandra on his arm, a twist of the dagger on top of his decade-long work to undermine King Diamandis on Kalyva.

He'd never been able to find the right woman though, and now that the plans were in place to take Diamandis down, it was the last little piece to the puzzle. A woman with no past, no history that could be unearthed. There was no way to prove, aside from actual DNA, that Al was *not* the princess.

Yes, luck was definitely on his side once again. Because he was close enough to all his plans that he could risk the bluff. A few days of media circuses and demands before any DNA test could be done.

As long as there was no body found—and Lysias was willing to risk the consequences as all his instincts told him there hadn't been—he would get *everything* he wanted. As long as Al cooperated.

So she would.

"I don't wish to learn *anything*," she said petulantly, wiping her mouth with the back of her hand.

So *much* work to do. "This isn't about your wishes, Alexandra."

She pointed the fork at him across the table. "Because you've kidnapped me."

"And what a terrible kidnapping it is. Eating a fine meal prepared by one of the best chefs in the country. A shower. A soft, warm place to sleep. The *horror.*"

"Oh, I'm not sleeping here."

"That you are," he said, his amusement fading. This was too important and her resistance would ruin his timeline. "You wish this to be a kidnapping, I can make it so. You are an integral part of my plan. I will pay you handsomely, but I will not tolerate your defection. I have lived my life focused only on revenge against one man, but trust when I say this." He leaned forward, needing to make sure she understood the gravity of this situation. "No one crosses me, Alexandra. No one."

CHAPTER FOUR

FEAR FLUTTERED IN Al's chest. She did not think Lysias would *hurt* her. As he kept pointing out, he'd saved her, and he was feeding her. And the doctor who had stitched her up had actually been kind. All of Lysias's staff had been efficient and kind as well.

Not to mention, the food was some of the best she'd ever tasted, and she *was* hungry. The dress she was wearing wasn't anything beautiful, but it was more comfortable than anything she'd ever worn. And the bath she'd taken—at the insistence of his staff—had been like nothing she'd ever experienced—warm and inviting and relaxing, even with the stab wound on her chest they'd had to work around.

She did not think Lysias was an *evil* man per se.

But she understood he only *cared* about his revenge. That she was only a tool in it, not something he was tending to because she mattered. He was making it very clear that if she got in the way of his revenge, she might be the next target of it.

And that *did* scare her a bit.

Al had enough self-preservation instinct to acknowledge, in her head, that going along with his plan, and taking her money and running when all was said and done, was likely better than escaping or trying to thwart him.

At least for now.

But she also didn't know how to simply sit back and accept that her circumstances had changed at the whim of a *billionaire*. That she was suddenly being bossed around by someone else.

Even if she went along with all this—enjoyed the food, a nice place to sleep, et cetera—that didn't mean she had to cede *all* control. He *needed* her after all. He'd said so himself.

"So, tell me about your plan," she said as irreverently as she could manage, with the delicious food and likely the painkillers twisting together to make her sleepy. But she was determined to stay awake. "So I can decide what parts I agree with. And what parts will need to be altered. Or require more compensation."

He raised an elegant eyebrow. She figured she was meant to wilt at that. But she held her head high. She was hardly intimidated by silence from an impressively gorgeous face.

Of course, when his surprise and condescension morphed into that slow, dangerous smile that caused dark, twisting sensations low in her stomach, she had to curl her hand into a fist underneath the table to remind herself not to let her unease…or interest show.

"First, we will attend a gala here in Athens," he said, turning his attention to his crystal wine glass. Al figured she could get a decent sum if she pawned just *one*. "I will introduce you as my fiancée to the eager media and crowd."

That got her attention. "You expect *me* to attend a gala as your *fiancée*?"

"You will have a considerable makeover." He met her gaze with all that amused gold. "Of course."

She tried not to scowl at him. Obviously, she would not fit into some billionaire *gala*. She wasn't sure even a "considerable" makeover would ever make it seem like she belonged. That didn't mean she *liked* it being pointed out to her with such obvious derision.

"Are you my fairy godmother, then?" she said sweetly.

"If you wish to see me as such, feel free." He waved a hand as unconcernedly as she was acting. Too bad she believed it on him.

"All right. So gala, introduce me—what does this have to do with the king of…wherever?"

"Kalyva. You will need to study up, as well as learn those table manners. After the gala, we will embark on a trip to my homeland. With the media in tow. I will claim that I have finally found the long-lost Princess Zandra so many thought—feared—dead. There will be a media circus. Lots of attention and distraction. The timing is perfect, as the king's spring ball will be held the weekend after we arrive, so there will already be much attention on the palace. The next morning is the annual council meeting, an integral part of my plan."

"I thought you needed to know about the body."

"It's true. My intel has not given me this information, but this is where Al comes in. You will find out while we tell all and sundry that Zandra is alive. My appearance and yours will be enough of a distraction to the kingdom that it will take some time to sort through. Even if there was a body, we'll be able to insist, for a few days, that it was an imposter's."

"Won't they be able to do tests to figure that out?"

"Yes, but such tests take time. If we are found out to be liars before I get what I want, I will say I was conned by a stunningly beautiful seductress." He flashed that alarmingly potent grin at her. "You will become Al, and no one will know what happened of said con artist pretending to be Zandra. However, if there is no body and never was, my plan will move forward. Regardless of the outcome, you shall receive your payment."

It was a ridiculous plan, made all the more ridiculous by her involvement. "Do you really think you can pass *me* off as a princess?"

"This is why the plan is perfect. You don't need to look the part of princess or act the part. You have enough a passing resemblance to be Zandra, who no one has seen for the past twenty years. And in my story, you have been suffering amnesia all these years. Secreted out of the palace to Greece, then raised by some poor farm family somewhere in a remote area of the country, with no education or training in royalty or wealth. Then, when your elderly parents passed, your grief led you to remember who you really are."

"That is some story," Al replied. "Who would buy it?"

"Everyone. Because I will ensure they do. You see, a fake princess has always been my plan, but I was never able to find someone who was quite right. You have no past to be uncovered. You can disappear into another identity should the need arise. You're well adept at all the sneaky things a job like this entails."

She did not know how this plan could possibly work. It was far-fetched at best. But she supposed if she held up her end of the bargain, it didn't matter if it was believed. She'd get paid either way. "What of those who are after me—after Al?"

"I will protect you, regardless of your identity, for as long as you are in my employ."

The word "protect" sent such an odd warmth cascading through her. She had never been protected. No one had ever cared...

But this was not about care. It was about revenge.

"So, when is this gala? How much time do I have to prepare?" She figured she'd need weeks, at the very least, to turn herself into someone who knew even how to *pretend* to be the fiancée of a billionaire. Particularly *this* billionaire.

"The gala is Friday. You have three days."

She laughed, though it was clear he wasn't joking. Just… "You're insane."

"No," he replied, sharp and foreboding. "I am determined."

Lysias answered the rest of Al's skeptical questions. And he had an answer for all of them. This had been his plan for so long, and it was finally coming together. Better than even he'd imagined.

Because she *was* perfect. No past for anyone to unearth. A passing resemblance to the Kalyvan royals. A willingness to pretend to be someone else for money, and the backbone to deceive whomever she wished.

Lysias was *mostly* certain the body of Princess Zandra had never been found, because the reports had always been that she'd been found with her brothers—which Lysias knew firsthand couldn't be true. He'd been in the palace that night, though he tried not to think too deeply on this. His theory was that the palace had planted that story so that the rumors and conspiracy theorists did not run amuck.

The rumors and whispers had anyway. Though, admittedly, not with the same fervor they might have otherwise. But enough, paired with the truth Lysias himself had witnessed, gave him this opportunity.

And he had his contingency plans in place on the off chance he was wrong. So, yes, the plan was perfect. So perfect he didn't even mind her questions.

But her eyelids began to droop, and before she'd even finished dessert, she'd fallen asleep. Right there at the table. Her head resting on her arm.

He wasn't sure how long he watched her careful, easy breathing. Wasn't sure *why* he watched it. Only that in sleep, she was just as compelling as awake. She did not look like a boy, or even the prickly young woman she'd been at dinner.

She reminded him of an old fairy-tale book his mother had read to him. A cast-off from the nursery of the royal children. Filled with old and faded illustrations of fairy sprites and brownies. Sweet and innocent-looking but full of mischief. Ready to lead you to danger if you were not careful.

Lysias was always careful.

Still, though he could have called his staff to take care of her, he did it himself. Moved over to her side of the table, lifted her from her chair. She barely made a sound, clearly exhausted by the day's events.

He carried her through the house, his footfall soft. She was so slight it was no hardship. He had set her up in the rooms just outside his private quarters—to keep his little flight risk close.

He nudged open the door and stepped inside. There was a light on, but only one, and it cast a soft glow. He made it to her bed and set her down on the mattress, then paused, glancing down at her. In the dim light, he had the flash of someone, something familiar. It stabbed through him like pain, so he shoved it away. He did not go back to those dark recesses of his mind, and whatever resemblance she had to anything back then was mere coincidence.

And would serve him well.

She didn't so much as whimper. She lay exactly where he put her, limp and helpless, the dress nothing but a baggy sack. And yet, something speared through him. A dark, possessive *want*.

She seemed unable to believe herself capable of becoming a princess, but Lysias knew everyone would believe it. She had the confidence, a kind of quiet beauty that could be teased out by all the tools women used. But even without her hair cut and fancily done makeup and a pretty gown, cleaned and fed, she had her own, unique beauty.

Her eyes fluttered opened, met his. But there was something far away about them, like she was still sleeping. Perhaps a waking dream?

"Am I safe here?" she murmured.

He heard someone else ask him that long ago. An old failure. An echo of an old loss amongst so many.

He said nothing to her. Made no assurances. He simply turned and strode out of the room, leaving all those distracting feelings, those old swirling memories behind.

And if he kept his distance the next three days, it was only because *he* had no experience turning a woman into a princess. He hired people who could do that. Who would polish her up to a pretty shine.

He had his staff pass along anything he thought she needed to know about Kalyva, hired an etiquette tutor for her so she might feel comfortable attending the ritzy charity gala. And he did not see her for three days.

The night of the gala, he readied himself in his rooms, ensuring with his man of affairs that all the details for their travel tomorrow was settled.

Tomorrow, he would be in Kalyva. Tomorrow, he would tell King Diamandis that the princess was alive.

And engaged to him.

Just the very thought of it all made Lysias smile as he straightened his tie. Tomorrow would be the beginning of all his revenge.

But first he needed to get through tonight. He strode through his house and down to the entryway. "Is she ready?" he asked the housekeeper.

"They are bringing her down."

"Excellent." Lysias didn't often have to wait on others, but he enjoyed the drama of an entrance. Why shouldn't she? His pretend bride. The perfect little tool of revenge.

It wasn't too much longer before he heard murmurs from the top of the grand marble staircase. She appeared, sandwiched by two members of his staff who seemed to be offering her last-minute advice as they moved forward.

She walked down the staircase at a careful glide. She was watching her feet, which gave the whole production a kind of authenticity. That of born princess raised farm girl plucked out of obscurity by a smitten billionaire.

In this moment, he didn't care for the idea he would need to pretend to be *smitten*, because the gown she wore outlined the body beneath all the baggy layers he'd seen her in. Her shoulders were bare, though the dress somehow came up high enough to cover her stitches so that no one would suspect she was the kind of woman who'd nearly been stabbed to death in a dangerous alley in Athens a few days prior.

The deep purple fabric of the gown swept around the slight curves of her body, the color of the dress making her skin warm, like she glowed from within. They'd trimmed and cleaned up her hair so that it curled gently under her chin and showed off the graceful, enticing curve of her neck.

Her face was made-up, though there was still something natural about it. Except the deep color of her painted lips.

Heat fisted into him, a blow he had not expected under any circumstances. As she reached the end of the staircase, her dark eyes lifted to meet his, and he found himself utterly speechless.

Lysias often accepted mistakes and failures as learning opportunities. A man did not get to his position without accepting that life would humble you, if you let it.

But he did not know what to do with *this* mistake.

Because Al had already drawn too many reactions out of him, but this one was worst of all.

For blinding seconds, he did not think of Kalyva, King Diamandis or everything he'd spent the last twenty years planning.

He only thought of what he might find if he peeled that dress away from her.

CHAPTER FIVE

AL STOOD AT the foot of the stairs. She stared at Lysias because he was looking at her with…hunger in his eyes.

She tried to tell herself she was imagining things. After all, she'd never been the object of anyone's desire. But she had also seen enough on the streets to recognize desire if she saw it.

And it was there in that golden gleam. Creating a matching claw of need within herself. She had wondered about sex before, but she had also known it was not in the cards for someone trying to disguise their gender.

Which she wasn't doing any longer. That thought spiraled through her like a strange, new, foreign kind of freedom. She could be a woman now—in whatever ways she wanted to be.

Then Lysias blinked, and everything in his eyes was gone. He moved forward, holding out his arm. She knew from her many meetings with the etiquette teacher that she was meant to lightly place her fingers on the crook of his arm.

She felt even more unsteady than she had trying to walk down the stairs in heels, though she had practiced that as much as she could. But something had shifted within her. A realization. An understanding.

Her life was different now. Not just because a payday that would change her life was within her reach, but also because she had this new identity. Alexandra. Woman. Fiancée. Princess.

She sucked in a breath and put her hand on his arm. Stepped forward in time with him as the possibilities swirled in her mind.

"You look perfect, Alexandra," he said, and though his eyes were cool and assessing now, there was a grit to his voice she had not heard from him before.

It was such a strange thing to find herself wanting to preen at the compliment. When she'd spent her entire life trying to keep her looks *under* the radar, so no one discovered her true sex. So no one paid too much attention to her while she spied.

But she liked it. She liked thinking that he might be right and that she was *perfect*.

She had to focus on the job, though. On the task. The payout. Which was no different than spying, except this was the endgame. She wanted to make Alexandra and safety *permanent*. And it was now within her grasp.

Unlike Lysias, who felt like a potential earthquake, which could happen out of nowhere and ruin *everything*. "Shouldn't you be calling me Zandra?" she asked, trying to speak the way she imagined her character would speak. Softly. With a kind of deference that was *definitely* not natural to her.

Lysias led her out the door and toward a sleek limousine waiting for them. "I think it'll be easier if we use Alexandra. We'll say that this is the name your adopted parents gave you and that you are currently most comfortable using it."

She nodded. Sensible. Smart. Why did he smell so good? How could a smell be so distracting?

She tried to get into the car elegantly, as many people had instructed her over the past few days, but she was sure she failed. She watched Lysias get in after her, all graceful and fluid movements.

"How did you learn?" she asked him. "All this..." She waved, frustrated that her vocabulary could not encompass that which she wished to ask. Frustrated he claimed to be *like* her but somehow fit into this world of wealth with such ease. "If you began life on the streets—"

"That is not where I *began* life. That is where I was *exiled*. I grew up in the palace of Kalyva."

She stared at him. Shocked by this simple admission. "But..."

"I told you, my parents worked for the king and queen. The *real* king and queen, not their disgusting excuse for a son. We lived in the palace. I was a servant's child and treated like one, of course, but I was always a curious boy. So I watched. I learned."

Every time he spoke of his childhood, she tried to picture him as a boy. And came up empty. She could only imagine the impossibly large man sitting next to her. Existing always as this beautiful example of what the human form could be.

They fell into silence as the limousine pulled away from the house and began the journey toward Athens. Al tried to keep her gaze on the window, but it kept finding its way back to Lysias.

"Where have you been?" She hadn't meant to ask him that. She hadn't meant to acknowledge she even noticed she hadn't seen him since that dinner three nights ago. Still, she couldn't take back the words, so she watched him and waited for an answer.

His face was blank—which was different than his revenge anger. Different even from the billionaire mask. This was something else. Something…dark. It had an uncomfortable mix of fear and sympathy entwined in her heart.

"Did my staff not take good care of you?" he asked offhandedly. Almost.

"You can't answer a question with a question."

"Ah, but I can. And do. And will."

Al frowned at him, but he didn't look her way. He settled himself into his seat and made a big production, *she thought*, of looking the handsome, relaxed billionaire on his way to any of his many important events.

She tried not to sigh, because nothing about Lysias mattered. The job, the payout mattered. She smoothed her hands down over her skirt. Everything was tight, which was a strange sensation. Showing off what she'd spent a lifetime hiding. But she'd seen herself in the mirror. She knew she looked pretty and sophisticated. It had been a shock to see her reflection in the mirror, and yet she liked it.

But it was still *strange*.

She was doing all right with the heels, though why any woman chose such torture devices was beyond her. She was more bothered by the fact she wanted to itch her hands through her hair as she had been expressly told not to so as not to ruin the sleek hairdo the stylist had spent nearly an hour creating.

Without warning, Lysias took her hand in his, and she jolted. At the way his touch sizzled through her. At how much effect he could have simply by taking her *hand*.

It was dangerous. But she'd spent too long dealing with danger not to revel in it a *little*.

"You are my fiancée. You must have a ring." And with that, he slid a cool piece of jewelry onto her finger.

She looked down at the sparkling stone. It looked like the kind of ring a billionaire would give his fiancée. Big and gaudy. She loved it. The way it sparkled. The way it felt. Which she knew wasn't the point. It wasn't *really* hers.

So she ripped her gaze from it and tried to focus

on the reality of the situation. "Maybe we should go over everything again," Al said, worrying her bottom lip between her teeth before she remembered her lipstick and stopped herself. She *liked* looking pretty, but it was an awful lot of work to remember how to maintain it all.

"There is nothing more to go over," Lysias said with a wave of his hand. "Tonight you need only to smile prettily for the cameras, stick close to me, and I will handle the rest. In fact, the less talking you do, the better. You are to be nothing but arm candy tonight."

Arm candy. She didn't like that term at all, but she supposed that is what *Alexandra* should strive to be. The quiet, happy billionaire's fiancée. "Do I know how to smile prettily?" Al wondered. "I have been given quite a few lessons over the past few days, but smiling was not one of them."

He finally turned his attention to her, and it was like a spotlight. She felt warmed, lit up. Like someone else.

"Well then, let us see a smile."

She tried to smile at him. It felt ridiculous, because she was attempting to look how an *Alexandra* might look. Or a princess. *Her* smile was that of a roguish street urchin. Not a sweet or even sophisticated woman. So she wasn't quite sure how to rearrange her features.

Lysias tutted and shook his head. "*That* is a grimace," he said, then reached out and touched her.

His long fingers stroked up her cheek. "Relax, *asteri mou*," he murmured. "Do not *try* so hard."

But she had to try hard. To breathe normally. To stay in this moment rather than be transported somewhere else by the heady drug that was his eyes on hers. Still, her body relaxed as if she had no choice. He was *willing* her through his touch, his gaze. The warmth that surrounded them convinced her to lean closer.

His smile in return felt genuine, soft almost, but the idea that Lysias Balaskas might be *soft* in any way was, of course, a fantasy.

"Better," he said, then dropped his hand.

She felt like drooping at the loss, but the car was pulling to a stop, and now she had to…pretend. Because that may have been pretend for him, but her reactions were not in any way an act.

They were real, and they were such a novelty, no matter how her brain warned her to be careful. Her brain insisted this might lead down a dangerous path, but the heady freedom of stepping out of the limo as a *woman*, as Lysias Balaskas's *fiancée*, seemed to eradicate the sensible voice in her head that had kept her alive for so long.

Inside the glittering soiree, Al did as she was told. Spoke little, kept to his side. It was easy to feign obedience because she was so far out of her depth in the glitz and glamour. Clutching to his side like a child to a mother felt safer than brazening it out alone.

She saw men she'd uncovered terrible things about.

She saw their wives still at their sides. It took some of the buzz of Lysias's closeness off.

How did these men still have their wealth, their power, their lives even after everything she'd brought to light about them?

She watched some of these men. Wondering if they'd look in her eyes and know who she was. When she saw no flickers of recognition, even as their gazes raked hungrily over her body, she wondered if it was the conceit that someone like her would never be in their hallowed halls of wealth and opulence. Or was it that she looked *that* different?

"Where are you, Alexandra?" Lysias murmured in her ear, that dangerous purr like a live wire through her system.

"Some of these men," she said, being careful not to point, to hold any of their lascivious glances. "I've exposed terrible things about them, but they are still…here. Not locked up. Not ostracized."

"Yes, power and influence can often make even your misdeeds someone else's problem," he said, as if it didn't bother him at all. But when she looked up at him, his gaze was fierce. "If you give me a list of names, I will ruin them all. Without a thought."

"Why?"

Lysias lifted a shoulder. "Why not?"

She supposed many of them were his adversaries in business. But… "What if you are friends with some of them?"

Lysias laughed. "Friends? None of these men are my friends. I do not have friends."

"Why not?" She could not have friends because she could not risk her secret, but it baffled her that a man of his power and influence would be similarly alone.

"Friends only ever end in betrayal, Alexandra. Best you know that now. Come, there's someone photographing the crowd of dancers. Let's join them so we will be splashed across websites and papers come morning."

He had that look on his face, much like when he spoke of his all-important revenge. Determination and the excitement of the hunt. He had a fierce one-track mind.

He'd experienced betrayal. Now wanted revenge *this* badly all these years later. He had been hurt as a young boy, no doubt, but Al wondered why twenty years hadn't dulled any of those old feelings.

Of course, she'd never had anyone to be betrayed by. These feelings were as foreign to her as protection or care.

Lysias pulled her into the soft, slow dance. She was dazzled by all the fabrics, the way they swished together. The way every woman glittered beautifully. It was such a strange world, and she was intrigued.

Lysias held her close, the hot, hard wall of him expertly moving her to the beat of the song. She'd had a few lessons, but not enough to do anything other than follow his lead.

He leaned his head down, his mouth grazing her ear. She knew this was all an act. He was hoping to be photographed. And yet, her body did not care *why*. Only that he was close. Only that one large hand was on the small of her back, that she could feel his breath on her skin.

"I will let it slip to someone at the very end of the night that your real name is Zandra Agonas," he whispered. "Someone who will immediately tell the press. Then they'll work themselves into a frenzy trying to get to the bottom of it. Some of them will likely arrive in Kalyva before even we do."

He smiled down at her—though it seemed wrong to call that curve of his mouth a smile. It was self-satisfied from a revenge well plotted. Hardly joy.

But it had that warm lick of desire twisting itself deep inside of her. So many women's eyes had followed him around the room tonight. She'd seen hands trail down his arms, lips lean in close to whisper.

Lysias had smiled at all these women, flirted with many, but he had always made it quite clear *she* was the object of his fascination this evening.

An act. Put upon. And yet, it was like becoming drunk, but it wasn't liquor. It was his attention, no matter how fake. She craved more and more. She wasn't sure she cared how authentic it was, as long as it spiraled inside of her like joy.

She wanted… In ways she'd never allowed herself to want. It hadn't been safe on the streets.

But she wasn't on the streets any longer. She let

her hand slide up his arm, curl around his neck. She let her fingers drag across the skin, soft here, like the ends of his hair. She trailed one finger along the line of his hair, then down his jaw.

He stiffened. Looked down at her—not in the disdain she feared, but in a kind of alarmed warning.

She didn't mind that at all. She was enjoying this too much. The harsh cheekbones, the sensuous mouth. She outlined it all with her finger, letting her body press more and more against him as he moved her. She felt the large, hard length of him pressed to her and shuddered out a sigh.

She wanted him. Because this seemed so fleeting. She wouldn't be a princess forever, and even if she escaped with her money at the end of this and built a new, quiet, safe life somewhere, it was hard to believe a desire like this would ever follow.

The hand on her back seemed to tighten. "You are playing a dangerous game, *asteri mou*." It was an order, a warning. Sharp. Dismissive…almost.

But when she looked from his mouth to his eyes, all that gold told a different story. So she smiled at him, with all she felt swirling inside of her shining through.

"Life is a dangerous game, Lysias. Why not play?"

CHAPTER SIX

THE BOLT OF need that slammed through Lysias was alarming. His little AI was dangerous, that was for certain. Who would have guessed that might extend past her abilities as a spy?

A hundred thoughts seemed to fight for purchase in his mind. Over the alarming fog of lust, of want. There *was* rational, sensible thought buried underneath those layers. But he struggled to bring them to the surface.

When he *never* struggled. Not anymore.

The music ended. He knew that much from the brush of bodies around them. So he used the hand on the small of her back to lead her away from the dance floor.

He had a plan, and he had to enact it. He could not be distracted by what she was offering. He knew exactly who he wished to slip the name *Princess Zandra Agonas* to, but he would have to tear his gaze from AI to find the other woman and that seemed impossible.

No. Nothing was impossible. Not for Lysias Balaskas. He searched the crowd, looking for his quarry. But Al and her wandering hands were a distraction. Enough of one that he led her out of the main room and into the hall. He moved her swiftly, taking her hand in his so it stopped its distracting trip down his shoulder blades.

He cornered her in a little alcove, where he was all in shadow, and a small shaft of light crossed over her face. He meant to lecture her. Tell her that some things were more important than a little flutter of lust, and she would need to learn this lesson.

But looking down at her, he couldn't seem to find any of those important words. There was only the knowing curve of her smile, the way her breath caught when he moved closer. That impossible burst of heat and need, unfamiliar in its intensity.

Where had this come from?

He meant to ask her—she must know. The words were on the tip of his tongue, he was sure of it. But her mouth was a dangerous, dark red. It glistened, beckoned to him, like a drug. She was a drug.

And he gave in.

He covered her mouth with his. It wasn't just heat here, but power. He smoothed his hands over the fabric of her dress, tight enough that it allowed him the delicious tour of her body as he used his to press her against the wall behind her.

He did not think of where he was, what his plan

had been. His only thought was that she felt like velvet, smelled like something dark, spicy, exotic.

She pressed against him, moaning into his mouth. Her hands clasped in his hair. It was wild. Reckless. And Lysias did not *mind* these things, usually quite enjoyed indulging in them, in the right setting.

But this was more… Just more. And it had to be stopped before he forgot his purpose. He pulled away from her, kept her pressed to that wall and held her at arm's length.

She looked up at him, those dark depths were hazy with lust. With need. And the need echoed so deep within, he nearly forgot himself and everything he was here for. Her breathing came in little pants, and…this was not the place, but that did not mean there was *no* place.

"Go wait for me in the car," he said, or growled, the fight for control taking over everything.

"But…"

"You want to play dangerous games…you will win dangerous prizes. I will have you in private, Alexandra."

She let out a sound. Maybe an *oh*. Her tongue darted out, pink against her now smudged lipstick. Then she nodded and turned away from him, walking toward the exit.

And he could only watch her. The confident swing of her hips, the beautiful, alluring slope of her shoulders. Then she looked over her shoulder at him, and when she caught him watching her…she smiled.

Another punch.

But he could not be laid flat by that blow, by all that crackled between them. He was too strong. Too determined. And while he was not against enjoying himself in the midst of his many plans, revenge would always come first.

Focus. The plan. Revenge. Bringing King Diamandis to his knees.

These reminders helped steady him. He found the hostess of the gala, offered thank-yous and goodbyes, and pretended to accidentally drop the name Zandra Agonas. Over-explained his error, until the woman's eyes were narrowed with suspicion.

And curiosity. He watched as her gaze moved across the crowd, land on a prominent journalist. Lysias kept the smile to himself as he said his final goodbye knowing that by morning wild stories about the maybe-not-dead Princess, and her connection to Lysias Balaskas, would be splashed everywhere.

Then he strode for the exit. For his car. For Alexandra.

His driver stood by the door, opened it for him with a nod. Lysias stood there on the curb, looking into the dim back seat where she sat. Looking right back at him. His driver stood by the door, waiting for Lysias to get in. "I can take it from here, Giorgio."

"As you wish, sir." The driver went back to the driver's side and Lysias stood where he was. Surveying the woman in his back seat.

This was not part of the plan. This woman. This

need. The danger he could feel encroaching around. He never let his focus waver. Never took on something that might risk what he needed to do.

But plans sometimes needed to be altered. They needed to accommodate changes in the landscape, and Alexandra was indeed a change.

It would not matter, he decided then and there. He took lovers as a matter of course. Enjoyed women, and sex. Surely this woman who'd grown up on the streets knew better than to look for something more than he would ever give.

He would have her. And his revenge. And when they were both over, settled and satisfied, they would part.

"Just so we are clear, I am not looking for any *real* wife."

She laughed, low and husky, arrowing right to his sex.

"I think I can see that about you, Lysias. I only want…" She trailed off, then shrugged those slim shoulders. "For so long, I have denied my wants, or had them denied for me, because I did not have the means to get them or because I had to hide who I was. Now I have the means, and I no longer need to hide. And I want. That is enough." She sat there for a moment, then raised an eyebrow. "Are you coming in?"

It felt like walking over a threshold that would change things, when he wished nothing to change now that he was here. Successful and poised on the cusp of his revenge, everything and all he'd wanted for twenty years.

But it was in the struggle of those twenty years—of his loss, of his exile, of his rise—he knew he could conquer whatever this was. Whatever threat she posed, he would simply not allow it to win.

Lysias Balaskas came out on top. Always. Forever.

He slid into the car, this back seat their own private oasis with the raised partition between driver and passengers. "You speak of these nebulous wants, Alexandra. Perhaps you should name a few, so as I am not confused."

She laughed again, and the enjoyment he got from this simple sound, the light in her eyes, might have startled him. If he could think beyond the need to taste such a laugh, such a woman.

"You are *never* confused, Lysias. But if you want to hear it, I don't mind. I want you to kiss me again."

He leaned forward but kept his mouth just out of reach even as she tilted her lips to his. He held this distance, a beat, and then another. She watched him, her breathing coming quicker, the pulse in her neck scrambling. He wanted to taste that spot of her neck, but he would be patient.

When he finally spoke, his words whispered over her lips, though he kept his hands to himself. So it was only heat that drew around her, their breaths comingling and nothing else.

"Is that all you want?" he asked, his voice a silken

whisper in the dark as the vehicle moved forward and they began to leave the lights of the city behind.

She sucked in an unsteady breath. If he was addled by the chemistry blooming between them, at least he was not alone.

"Touch me," she said. Demanded, actually.

Which would not do. "Ah, but I do not take orders from anyone, *asteri mou*."

"And I do not *ask* for anything, *leventi mou*. I simply take it." She fisted her hand in his tie and pulled his mouth to hers. Fire. Need.

He could have avoided it, of course. She *was* strong, but no match for him. But he enjoyed her strength, her demands. That she would grab onto whatever power she could scrabble together.

It didn't matter. Because she would be begging him for more before all was said and done.

So he kissed her. Tasted her deep and allowed himself, in the world of this car, to forget everything else. For these brief moments, she was all that existed. And he lost himself in her.

She was dark and sweet, wild and fearless. An earthquake. A challenge to all his previously held beliefs, and yet he welcomed it. Weathered it. Absorbed it all. And created his own response. So that she was quaking in his arms.

He slid his hands up her legs. Slight, but strong. He pushed the fabric of her skirt up and away. In the dark of the back seat, she was but a shadow. A rustle. A whisper. She could have been a phantom.

Except she was warm and real, and he wanted more. All. He slid his hands beneath her underwear, found the center of her. Where she was wet and ready for him. He teased her with his fingers, the drugging scent of her arousal filling the car.

He wanted her more than he could remember wanting anything. Which was dangerous, because he'd only wanted revenge before. Too dangerous to feel this...under her spell. So he took what power he could. He stopped his ministrations.

"Thank me." When she stilled and her eyes flew to his in the dim light, he smiled. "For saving your life."

Her mouth opened, but it seemed to take her quite a bit of time to find her voice. Still, he held himself exactly where he was, his fingers within the tight heat of her, still.

He could see the war play out over her face. Which did she want more? Her pride? Or him. Eventually, lust won. "Th-thank you," she whispered. And he didn't know if she meant it.

He wasn't sure he cared. He touched her, over and over again, until she was writhing once more. He watched what little of her face he could see change from wonder to desperation. Shock to ecstasy. He took his time, enjoying the swell of her climax, the sounds of her desire throbbing through him—pleasure and the torturous pain of holding himself back.

She came apart so beautifully, his name on her

lips, there in the dim light of the limousine. What a surprise she was. What a glorious, delicious surprise.

"Lysias," she said, ragged and weak. For him. Because of him.

He removed his hand from underneath her dress, kissed down the elegant curve of her neck. He tasted her there, just where he'd wanted to. Where she smelled of something secretive and uniquely her. "Yes?"

He drew back, studied her shadowed face. She seemed to be struggling with something.

He smiled at her. "If you want more, you will have to ask nicely." But he pulled her dress back down over her legs because he realized the car had come to a stop.

"Ask…" She straightened herself as Giorgio opened the back door. Lysias slid out, quite pleased with himself, no matter how hard he was for her. How his body was tormented by all this unspent desire.

He held out his arm, watched expressions chase over her face before she finally placed her hand on it. She allowed him to lead her inside and she said nothing.

Darkly amused with her, and himself, Lysias walked her all the way upstairs. Up to her bedroom door. He even offered her a little bow, as if she really was a princess.

"Good evening, Alexandra."

She blinked. Once. Then her eyes narrowed. "You're really going to make me beg you?"

"Who said anything about begging? I only said you had to ask nicely. Though, I also appreciate begging. And reward it handsomely."

"And what happened in the car wasn't nice enough?"

"Nice for *you*." He shrugged lazily, then turned away from her. He walked down the hall toward his own bedroom door. Because surely, she would give in. Surely...

"Please," she said, on a quiet mutter. Perhaps even through gritted teeth.

He turned to her, raised an eyebrow, with far too much distance between them. But she would always be the one to give in. Never him. "Please what?"

She hesitated, which surprised him. But it was only a moment's worth, and then she was crossing the hall to him. All determination and fire.

"I want you. All of you." She slid her arms around his neck, pressing that delicate body to his much larger one. Her dark eyes an enchantment all their own. "Show everything to me, Lysias. *Please*."

CHAPTER SEVEN

AL DID NOT believe in retreat. She also knew that good never lasted, so she had to grab what opportunities were within her reach without hesitation.

She didn't *relish* asking, let alone nicely, when she was so used to taking. But something about the way Lysias looked at her when she said please—that golden gleam in his eyes leapt like a flame. And something hot and dangerous grew inside of her.

Who knew when she might be able to have this? She had almost died earlier this week. She had struggled for so long up to this moment. Why not finally live in all the ways she hadn't been able to?

Enjoy the gowns, the excess and this man. This desire. Take it all, experience it all, while she could.

She lifted to her toes, pressed her mouth to his. His hands, which had remained frustratingly at his sides, now moved up to cup her face, angle her head differently. He took the kiss deeper, wilder, like he had in the car. She wanted everything she'd felt then, but more.

She wanted her hands on *his* body. She wanted to feel what she could do to *him*.

He pulled her down the hall, and she was so unused to the heels that she nearly tripped. But he held her upright, leading her into his bedroom with a single-minded purpose. She stepped inside, taking it all in. The wealth, the beauty, this shocking and wondrous feeling inside of her. The way the sound of the door closing behind her filled her with anticipation and want.

The room she'd stayed in was beautiful, more luxurious than anything she'd ever seen, but his was remarkable. Not just the space but how comfortable everything looked. How warm and soft.

But when he pressed his mouth to the back of her neck, she could not have cared less about the big windows with their view of the night sky or the soft give of the plush carpet underneath her heels.

She only cared about the sensations his mouth, his hands could create in her. No wonder people did stupid things for this. *This* was a drug worth risking for. She wanted to turn, but his fingers brushed the top of her dress, and she heard and felt him pull the zipper down. Until the dress slithered down and pooled at her feet.

The dress had not allowed her to wear anything underneath it up top, and though her breasts were small, it was strange not to have them bound. She brought her arms up to cover herself reflexively, even as she stepped out of the dress, back still toward him.

"Face me, Alexandra."

Yes, she was Alexandra now. A woman. A powerful woman. With money and position and whatever she wanted. Including a lover. *This* lover. So she turned, though an old ingrained habit or shame or *something* had her keeping her arms over her bare chest.

He shook his head and reached forward, taking her by the wrists, but the touch was so gentle it was like he barely held her at all. And when he pulled her hands away from her breasts, she didn't even think to fight him. Not with the way his gaze raked over her. Hungry.

"How you have hidden such beauty is beyond me," he murmured. His thumb brushed over one darkened peak, and pleasure shot through her from that point to the aching center of her.

"Lysias." She didn't know what to say. What to ask for. She understood sex as a kind of impartial bystander—she had lived on the streets too long not to hear how people spoke of it, witness what people would do for it. She understood, too, that there were many different uses. That it could be unwanted, transactional, but also she knew that some people sought it out. The pleasure, the release. The wild rush of it all.

She wanted that. With him. Here and now and for as long as they could, because it would not last, this wild, desperate feeling. Nothing this wonderful ever did.

"What is it you want from me, *asteri mou*? Do you wish me to touch you again, to watch you fall apart here in the light?"

"Yes. No. I…" She wanted everything and had no vocabulary for all her wants.

"Or perhaps I should taste you," he continued, maneuvering her deeper into the room until the back of her knees hit the bed, and she found herself seated.

Lysias kneeling before her, as he spread her legs apart.

She opened her mouth with a thought to say something. Anything. But she could only stare, magnetized as he pulled her panties from her, leaned forward and, with no preamble, licked deep within her.

She might have bolted off the bed, if he'd not hooked his arms around her legs. Holding her in place. His strength felt like a safe haven, even as new needs clawed at her, and pleasure climbed and climbed into its explosive peak.

When she managed to open her eyes, she was sprawled out on his bed, completely naked. And he stood at the foot of the bed, completely clothed. The only sign he'd done anything untoward was his slightly disheveled hair and the smudge of lipstick—*her* lipstick—on his jaw.

She had the strangest desire to put her mark all over him.

She pointed at him. "Now you. Take off your

clothes." Because this wasn't fair, and she wanted to see him. Needed to see under all that polish.

He raised a dark brow. "I thought we had established that I do not like to be demanded about." But he loosened his tie, his golden gaze holding hers as he slowly pulled it from his shirt.

Her heart thundered in her chest, and everywhere he'd touched—with his hands, with his mouth—throbbed with the desire to feel him. Naked against her.

So she moved to the end of the bed and onto her knees on the mattress. She did not ask or plead. She reached out and began to unbutton his shirt. She pressed a kiss on his chest for each undone button, the faint smudges of whatever lipstick she had left giving her a darkly sensual satisfaction.

When she reached the end, the buckle of his belt, she looked up at him through her eyelashes and slowly unhooked then pulled it out of the belt loops. And though she fumbled as she undid his button of his pants, faltered for a moment with the zipper, she could not seem to tear her gaze from him.

Until she spread apart the fabric of his pants and was met with the large evidence of his arousal. She sucked in a breath, feelings and sensations such a powerful cyclone in her mind she had no fully formed thoughts at all.

Only need. She tugged his boxers down so that he was free. She smoothed her hand down the silky, hard length of him. Need and satisfaction shot through her at the noise he made, a harsh sucked-in breath.

She managed to look up at him again. So handsome, like a statue. But he was made of muscle and skin. Blood pumped through his veins, and his heart beat fast. She was sure she could reach out and feel it do so through his chest.

Because it felt as if hers was doing exactly that. And she found herself stuck, because she did not know what to do. She did not wish to let on that she was inexperienced. She wanted only to be the Alexandra he'd turned her into.

He fitted his hand over her cheek, then led her head forward. She knew what he wanted, and it became what she wanted. To take him deep within her mouth. The slick friction, the salty taste of him. She absorbed the sound of his groan, his shattered breathing, and she wanted to be the reason he fell apart.

But he pulled her back, his golden eyes so fierce she was nearly afraid she'd done something wrong.

"Lay down," he ordered.

She no longer cared who ordered who. If she had to beg or plead. Something clawed at her from inside and the only escape was him. Inside of her.

He rolled a condom on, and Al refused to be afraid. That was how a woman such as her got through any unknown situation. Believing you belonged in it. Believing you could handle anything.

And then he was on top of her, careful around her wound. Heavy and strong. Her protector. The

man who had saved her. Who had given her pleasure, and now this.

Poised at her entrance, and she had no fear. Not
here. Not with him. Not as he slid inside of her, with
inexorable pressure and determination.

She had heard stories of varying experiences.
That there was pain or discomfort or only glory.
That it depended on the man, his size or that foolish
thing called love.

She found her experience somewhere in the middle of all that noise. He was so large, and it felt as
though she would never accommodate him. And
yet there was pleasure everywhere else. And as he
moved within her, as she moved against him not
knowing what else to do with the pressure and the
need, any mild pain, any discomfort melted away.

And then there was only this, where they joined,
the little world of ecstasy, of rising tides of pleasure,
one after the next. His hands were everywhere, his
mouth devoured her, and deep within, he moved.
Closer and closer to an edge she now recognized,
now knew, now craved.

She sobbed his name, needing something from
him she did not know how to express. Except his
name. Over and over again. Until the world upended
in a magical crash of ecstasy.

On one last thrust, he crushed her to him, power
and passion in one explosion before they both fell
limp together on the bed. For stunning moments, they
breathed in time, slowly coming back to themselves.

This real world where she would now have to deal with the consequences of her wants. Except, what was so bad about this? It was an enjoyment for both of them. He'd made it clear there would be no union, and she knew that she had some new life far away from this one in her future once she helped him with his revenge and was paid.

Besides, finding enjoyment in each other would suit the role they had to play of an engaged couple. Why would there be an ounce of regret?

He moved off her, saying nothing. He disappeared into the bathroom, and when he returned, he stood in the doorway between bedroom and bathroom. He looked angry, which she could not understand.

"You should have told me," he said, his voice tight, that golden gaze of his hard.

She didn't see the point in doing anything other than lay in the middle of his bed, enjoying the soft linens and mattress beneath her as the remnants of her pleasure petered out pleasantly. "Told you what?"

"That you have had no lovers before me."

She wrinkled her nose at him, trying to make sense of him. "Why?"

"So I could have been more…careful."

She stretched out her arms, letting out a contented, satisfied sigh. "No worries. I quite enjoyed myself." Which was an understatement, but maybe understatements were safer when he looked so stormy, standing so very far away.

When he said nothing and stayed exactly where

he was for long, tense moments, she finally rolled over onto her stomach so she could stare at him. "Lysias, I don't understand why this bothers you. I knew what I was doing. I asked for it. I even said please, if you recall."

Something ticked in his jaw. But even better, she saw the flare of desire at the recollection in his eyes.

"Would you like me to leave?" she asked, smiling cheerfully at him. "I'm afraid you'll have to say please."

He made a noise, maybe a growl, then stalked over to the bed. But he did not join her on it, did not gather her into his arms with a punishing kiss as she'd half hoped. He stood there looking like some kind of ancient warlord she'd wronged.

Which she did not hate as much as she probably should.

"Do not forget, Alexandra. I am in charge. No matter what happens in the bedroom, my revenge is all I care about."

"And I do not care about your revenge at all," she said, enjoying her flippancy in response to his intensity. "But I would very much like to do that again. Shall I beg?"

Lysias could not say what bothered him about the realization she'd been an innocent. Perhaps that it had never occurred to him she might be. That she likely *had* to be, as she'd been hiding who she truly was for most of her life.

He did not, as a rule, dally with virgins who were likely to get…ideas about such things. Mountains out of molehills and such. No matter how mountainous this had felt.

And she had the audacity to lay there on his bed, naked and sheer perfection, smiling at him as if she were the queen of his world.

Perhaps what bothered him was that she surprised him. That he could not predict her. Read her or understand her.

Except in the fact that she wanted him as much as he wanted her. Even now, when they should be sated and exhausted.

So he did not send her away. He kept her in his bed. Another rule broken, but they *were* pretending to be engaged. They would share a bed in Kalyva, and Kalyva had to be what he focused on. They would leave in the morning. To begin all the plans for his revenge.

But the strangest thing happened in the middle of the night. He woke, as he often did, torn from a nightmare that was mostly memory, though sometimes twisted with monsters and figments of his childhood imagination.

He expected that he might have wakened her, cursing himself for the weakness of allowing her to share his bed.

When he looked over at her, ready to lecture or tell her to leave, she was indeed awake. But she was sitting up in almost a mirror of the same position he found himself in. Hands pressed to the mattress, sheet twisted about her body, her hair plastered in sweat and sharp breaths coming in terrified pants.

Their gazes met and held as their breathing evened out. He realized, somewhere in his sleep addled mind, that she had been having her own nightmare.

It speared through him, this realization. That they might have things in common. That they might understand each other, when he did not wish to be understood. He only wished to find vindication.

He should pay her for her services at the gala and then tell her to go. He would find a different Princess Zandra. One who did not threaten *everything*.

But they were too far gone in the plan. She was his Alexandra, the tool he would use for his revenge.

And revenge was the only thing that mattered. Perhaps she might come to understand pieces of him because she knew the hard truths of life. But this would not become *more*, even if he was her first. She had said it herself, she only wanted to enjoy her wants.

She would not weave fairy tales.

He was determined, even as they headed for the island kingdom of Kalyva the next morning.

Where kings and dead princesses and the haunted history of his past waited for them.

CHAPTER EIGHT

THE BOAT RIDE was uneventful. The boat, of course, a luxurious vessel that sped through the beautiful Aegean Sea with ease and grace.

That did nothing to ease Al's queasy stomach. She was coming to find she much preferred land.

"Don't tell me you're seasick, Alexandra," Lysias said, taking a seat next to her on the deck—the only place she could seem to handle the movement, with the cool air slapping against her face.

"I am definitely not sea *well*," she replied, pressing her cheek to the cool railing. "Mark me down as not a fan of boats."

"It is a *yacht*."

She shrugged. "It is all the same to me."

"Well, never fear. Land is near." He pointed out across the blinding blue. She saw it then. The island in the distance. The gray craggy offering of stone, the colorful parade of boxes that must be buildings, against the contrasting white of the beach and what could only be the palace at the very top of the slope of land in the middle of the sea.

Al watched it as it got closer and closer, but it did nothing to soothe the unease in her stomach. So she looked at Lysias.

They had said nothing to each other last night when she'd woken to find him also awake. She was certain he must have had a nightmare just like she had. Instead, once their breathing had evened, they'd found a silent solace in each other's bodies. And then gone back to sleep.

She hadn't wanted to face the darkness of her dreams in that bed, where she'd felt safer than she'd ever felt. But here on this boat... "What do you dream of, Lysias?" she asked him. Already knowing he would turn the question around on her.

"Many things, naturally. What do you dream of, Alexandra?"

She sighed. "I don't know. It is always in shadow. Screams and pain and confusion. A hand reaching out to save me, and then variations of a theme of losing that savior from there." She shrugged. She'd often been embarrassed by having nightmares at her age, and it was hard to shake that feeling, but Lysias had them too. Maybe that meant she was not so very different.

And she just needed to know that she was not alone. That he might understand. She reached across to him, curled her fingers around his arm. "Tell me. Please."

He did not look at her, but he also did not dislodge her hand. He simply squinted behind his sunglasses at the approaching island, the sun painting him a stunning, golden figure in the midst of all this blue and white.

"Memories mixed with monsters. But once my revenge is complete, I will conquer them the same as I will conquer my old friend."

"This king was your *friend*?"

"I thought he was, anyway. But it is of no matter. We are enemies now. And once I have vanquished my enemy, all will be put behind me."

"You're sure of this?"

He glanced at her, though the glasses hid any hint at what expression might be in his eyes. "Absolutely."

She wondered if she would ever have the confidence to believe she could vanquish her subconscious coming out in dreams. When, if she had that power, she would have conquered it already. Really, men were such ridiculous creatures.

The boat pulled up to a dock, and Lysias threaded his fingers with hers as they waited for his staff to secure the boat and ramp that would allow them to disembark.

Al studied his hand in hers. It felt oddly familiar, here in this place.

She shook that strange thought away and surveyed the island before her. It looked cheerful on the sunny, warm morning, and yet she did not find herself *cheered*. She felt cold.

It was nerves, she supposed. Lysias said he had no doubts the king would be there to greet them, and their act must begin at once.

She had to pretend to be the man's sister. *Dead* sister. It seemed a bit cruel, but she knew life was cruel. It had been to her *and* Lysias. Perhaps it had been to the king as well, but he was a *king*. He could no doubt weather it.

She had been forced to scramble, to fend for herself at too young an age—and so had Lysias. Perhaps it was dangerous to view herself on the same team as Lysias, but it was temporary. And if they could trust one another, it would serve their purposes at deceiving the king—which would lead to her payment.

Lysias drew her down the ramp to land, and Al worked very hard to look her part. The wide-eyed princess who'd only just remembered who she was. The, if not sophisticated, graceful and *feminine* fiancée to Lysias Balaskas.

"Ah, home," he said, but with a sharp edge. Certainly not a warm homecoming, what with revenge clearly holding his whole mind in its grip.

It *was* a beautiful little jewel of an island. Al had never been out of Athens, not that she could recall, but she'd seen the pictures and paintings of all the beautiful Greek islands and knew people sought them out.

The air was warm and smelled of the sea. And just beyond the docks, there was a small crowd. Everyone was dressed in black except one man, who wore black and red and stood on a kind of platform that led to a large official-looking car on the road beyond the beach.

He was also the only one without a gun.

Beyond him were buildings—homes and shops, she supposed—but then, high on the hill, a bright white building—devoid of any and all color against the dark blue of the sky. Stone turrets, stout and tall, reached up into all that blue just as domed spires did. It was beautiful, clearly old and important.

Something like pain sliced through her. She had a sudden bolt of panic. She stepped backward, thinking only she needed to run, but she was met by the hard wall of Lysias himself.

"What is it?" he asked. She supposed she was imagining any true concern in his tone. This was an act, after all.

"I…" She didn't know how to explain it. This feeling of dread that seemed to coil around her heart and squeeze. "I don't like the look of this place."

"Kalyva is beautiful, Alexandra."

"Yes." It was. Objectively. This wasn't about beauty though. It was about a feeling. Deep in her gut. The feeling she had always listened to on the street. The one that had kept her alive. She didn't feel safe here. She didn't feel right.

But Lysias was behind her, moving her forward. He was her protector. Maybe that was temporary, but for now, she would take it. She would relax within that knowledge. Or try.

They moved toward the man who stood on the road that was lifted above the beach and docks. He looked down at them as if they were bugs. Yet there was something about him... Al tried to breathe through the scrambled racing of her heart. Panic twined around her lungs. Squeezing.

She wanted to run. *Had* to. But Lysias held her there.

"You are either very brave or very foolish," the man said in clipped tones once Lysias came to a stop not far from him. The man was clearly ignoring her and talking specifically to Lysias.

Who flashed his fake billionaire smile. "Both, likely. And I know you will not fall to your knees and thank me just yet, though you should, but I have brought your sister back to you, Your Majesty. You are most welcome."

Lysias stared at King Diamandis, and yet his attention was fractured because Alexandra was acting so strangely next to him. Skittish and tense. Perhaps he should have let her arrive as Al, an identity she was more comfortable with.

But that was ridiculous. How she felt, how comfortable she was, it was all immaterial to his goals. She would be paid handsomely for her subterfuge, and so there was no need to *protect* her.

"The rumors are swirling, as you have no doubt ensured," the king said. "But, as my people have told everyone who has come sniffing thus far, the princess died when the rest of my siblings did."

It was strange to stand here in what he still considered his homeland, though he'd lived in Athens now longer than he'd been a boy here. Because nothing had changed except the man before him. Who was no longer a boy of fourteen, but now a man. A king.

Twenty years between then and now. Between friends and enemies.

Because Diamandis *had* been his friend. Lysias had considered this man a brother, though he'd known Diamandis's standing much more important than his own. But Diamandis had never made him feel it.

Until that night.

And Lysias could have forgiven Diamandis much. His own exile, certainly. But he would never forgive the man responsible for his parents' deaths, without even their dignity in that death. Buried as traitors, accomplices to murder. With nothing.

So Lysias smiled wider. "Ah, yes, and it's a neat little lie, but it *is* a lie." Lysias widened his smile that he did not feel. "I should know. I was there."

There was a beat where Diamandis looked at him with such cold hatred, Lysias felt the strange need to pull Al behind him. Protect her from the destruction he wanted to enact here.

"You will come to the palace," the king ordered, with the flick of a wrist. His armed men began to move forward. Toward Lysias. Toward Al. Lysias held on to her.

"We have secured our own accommodations, of course," Lysias replied with the kind of fake deference that had Diamandis scowling down at him. "Our own transportation as well... But if you'd like to show your sister around the palace, we would be happy to meet you there this evening. Perhaps a nice din—"

"Enough." Temper flashed on Diamandis's face, but the man *had* changed in twenty years. Not just moving into adulthood, into being king. It seemed he'd finally learned to control his disastrous temper. "You will come to the palace. We will discuss all of this there. You can come of your own free will, or you can be dragged." He nodded toward the little army of guards that were even now surrounding them.

Lysias was not surprised. He knew what a threat he was to his old *friend*. Still, he didn't relish Alexandra being part of this. But she had a role to play. So Lysias's smile did not change.

Nor did he act *threatened*.

"So, you would make us prisoners?" Lysias replied, feigning surprise. "This seems extreme, Diamandis."

"The appropriate term is *Your Majesty*, as you well know, Mr. Balaskas."

"Come, Diamandis. Let us not pretend we don't know one another. Think of all we have shared."

Lysias thought of it. Too often. And how all his youthful innocence had been betrayed.

"I wish I'd *never* known you," Diamandis spat. "You may use your own transportation, but have no fear. My guards will accompany you to the palace. Immediately."

Lysias lifted a negligent shoulder. "If it's so important to you, *Your Majesty*, we are happy to oblige." He even gave a little bow, because he knew Diamandis would see the gesture as flaunting, not deferential.

The king whirled away, muttering something to his guards before he was led back to his vehicle. The guards that remained for him did not bother Lysias in the least, as it all went to plan. He smiled winsomely at the guards, leading Alexandra to where one of his own employees waited next to the car he would use on Kalyva.

She looked perfect here. The dress she wore was elegant but suited for the warm temperatures—the top hooked to the skirt with little ties—offering tempting little glimpses of her golden skin. The hairdresser had done something with her hair so that it curled, looking a bit wild and yet beautifully suited to the smoky makeup on her face.

And he wished he could take her somewhere else. Somewhere decadent and safe where she could…

He blinked at the odd course of his thoughts. There was nowhere else. There was only revenge.

He opened the passenger side door for Alexandra

himself, then got into the driver's side. A heavy-duty
car pulled out in front of him, and another waited
behind. The king's little cavalcade.

He flicked a glance at Alexandra as he drove toward the palace. She was staring up the hill at the
estate with a furrow across her brow and a frown
on her face. He could not say he fully understood
her reaction to this place. Was she nervous? Afraid?
Having second thoughts?

It did not matter, as he would not tolerate a de-
viation to his plan. And still the words tumbled out.

"You have been quiet."

"I don't like this place," she said plainly. "Everything gives me a bad feeling, and I have always relied
on those feelings to keep me safe. It's very…unsettling
to not be able to listen to them now."

"Well, there is certainly danger to be found here.
And this island—the palace specifically—was the
site of many an atrocity. So, perhaps your feelings
are valid, but they do not change what we must do."

"No, I know." She frowned deeper. "It isn't that
I'm regretting anything or thinking of backing out.
It's just, as I said, unsettling." She straightened her
shoulders and seemed to stare down the palace like
she could scowl it into obedience. "I'm sure I will
get over it."

Something strange moved through him as he
drove over the bridge that led up to the palace, following the guard's car ahead of him. It was like a
warmth. He supposed, if pressed to define it, he

might have called it *pride*, that she would be so determined to overcome her discomfort.

The car in front of him rolled to a stop at one of the back entrances. Lysias had to laugh, if darkly. The servant's entrance. He was very familiar with *this* part of the castle. It was meant to be an insult, no doubt, but if Diamandis was bothering with insult, he knew Lysias was a threat.

The guards in both cars began to get out, so Lysias leaned over to Alexandra and spoke quietly.

"I believe the king will want us to stay in the palace. He'll want to keep us close and under careful guard. I will put up a *small* fight, but in the end, I'll let him have his way. This will allow you to prowl the palace as Al, if necessary."

Alexandra studied him with wide eyes he couldn't read, but she eventually gave him a nod. Then the vehicle doors were opened for them. And Lysias had to put on the role of careless billionaire, who truly believed Alexandra a princess.

He stepped out, made a few irreverent quips, then offered his hand to Alexandra when they met in front of the car. The guards marched them up to and then inside the doors.

So many painful memories. Most he'd worked very hard to forget. But they crowded in the shadows, slithered around him. And the worst part, they weren't all of *that* night. There were warmer ones. Of his parents. Of his friendship with Diamandis.

Of the kindness of the king and queen. Those were worse than the nightmare reality of bloody coups.

He looked over at Alexandra as they were lead away from the servant's area and more toward the royal wing. Something darker, more hidden tried to claw forward as he caught a glimpse of her profile against the background of the ancient marbled palace. Time wanted to warp, send him back into old terror.

But he wouldn't go there. He never went there. Except in dreams.

And this was no dream. Only his long-awaited revenge finally within his grasp.

CHAPTER NINE

AL TRIED VERY hard to shake off the feelings of unease. But every step they took deeper into the palace, flanked by intimidating men in military-looking gear, the anxiety coiled so tight she worried she wouldn't be able to pretend anything at all.

She looked over at Lysias. His gaze was forward as they walked, his expression a kind of blankness that reminded her of last night. When she'd woken terrified and breathless and turned to see him the same.

"You may wait here," one of the guards said outside giant ornate doors. They depicted some kind of ancient scene in golds and bronze and bright blue paint. Alexandra studied the images, tried to make sense of them.

"The first battle of Kalyva," Lysias said loudly. "Perhaps it will bring back some more of your memory if I explain it to you."

"It seems familiar," Al said, reaching out to touch a golden horse with its legs reared. And that wasn't a lie. But she was an adept enough liar to find as much truth in her falsities as she could. "But so many of my memories are a jumble."

Lysias put his hands over hers, drew her index finger forward to trace the horse. "Then allow me to help." He told her a story about two warring groups of ancient warriors—one made for battle and one that found battle by necessity. He weaved it so it sounded more fairy tale, more myth, than actual historic episode.

And she was rapt, not sure which side she rooted for or which side would come out on top. He told the story with such relish she turned her gaze from the door's art to him. The harsh profile, the slight curve of his lips, the deep tenor of his voice.

She felt all that heat from last night and something else. More tender. Like when she'd looked over to find him awake from a nightmare as well and wanted to soothe him in some way.

He glanced at her in the midst of a sentence, and either he trailed off, or she stopped listening. Amidst all her fear and anxiety and discomfort here, one thing was very clear in this moment.

Lysias had not changed. She wanted his mouth on hers again, to feel him inside her. No matter how she felt about Kalyva or the palace, she wanted him all the same.

The doors opened abruptly, and Al assumed she must have been so startled by her own reactions to him that she was only imagining Lysias looked as startled by the interruption as she felt. Because, in a blink, he was facing down the king with that laissez-faire smile. And golden daggers in his eyes.

"Sit," the king ordered, pointing to some delicate-looking chairs in front of a large intimidating desk. The room was some kind of office, likely the king's office. Alexandra took in the plush rugs, the elaborate window treatments. Every wall had panels of art much like the door, depicting different scenes—she assumed of the history of the royals.

Lysias drew her forward and took a seat on a small settee, pulling her down to sit next to him. She was glad for his proximity, for his lead. It felt a bit like an anchor in the midst of all this unfamiliar discomfort.

The king did not sit behind his desk. He came to stand in front of it, glaring down at them impressively. He was severe, his features dark. His clothes matched his face, all perfect crisp lines and shiny buttons, as though nothing would dare wrinkle or tarnish under his watch. He *looked* like a king, if a little on the young side to preside over an entire country.

Lysias had said she had enough resemblance to the royal family they might believe a connection were true. She stared at the king, but she saw very little, aside from coloring, that might connect them. Of course, she'd never spent much time studying her own face.

"If you wish to push this farce," the king said. "We only have to do a DNA test to prove you wrong."

"Naturally," Lysias replied, resting his ankle on his knee, and flicking imaginary lint from his pants. "Do you think I would really bring you a fake, knowing how easy it would be to prove me wrong?" He turned to exchange an amused look with Al. "I told you he would be suspicious, but we will get through to him."

She forced her mouth to curve and nod at Lysias. She was afraid she wouldn't be able to sound just right yet. She didn't have the reserves she needed to be Alexandra, lost princess.

"I hope you both understand that I don't have to entertain this. You are not welcome here, Lysias. You were exiled. I can have you tossed right back out or in a cell or even killed."

"You can do all those things, certainly. But can you look at this woman here and tell me you do not see the resemblance? The evidence of your own blood in her veins?"

The king did not look at her. She realized it was purposeful. He *would* not look at her. He focused on Lysias and tossed some more threats around, while Lysias had an answer for everything. Their voices felt like thunder rumbles, distant and incomprehensible, so she got up without fully thinking the movement through.

They argued and she went to stand at the window to get away from the anger in the room—no matter how calm they tried to sound. She looked out at the blue of the sea, the white of the sand, the people walking down there, small and disconnected from the storm raging inside here.

Why did it all feel so familiar?

She reached out, touched the wall next to the window. Her fingers traced the wallpaper design, and she studied the art panel next to the window. This did not appear to be a depiction of battle but of a coronation.

She studied it—not just the art but the frame of the panel around it. She knew it wasn't familiar, as she'd never been here. But she'd seen something like it…somewhere. It must have been in her early spying days. Some of those jobs ran together on the heady mix of fear and the thrill of success.

That had to be it.

She reached out, felt around the little framed edge, found the button…and pressed. A door popped open with a loud *snick*.

She stood there looking at the dark interior behind the door for she didn't know how long. She didn't know what was happening to her, what strange sensations were coursing through her. So she turned to Lysias, her protector. Her anchor.

He stood now, next to the king, and both men stared at her as if she'd sprouted wings and flown. She felt a bit detached, as if she *had* flown away. It didn't fully make sense, even to her. But she supposed she was used to such things. Finding hideaways and secrets in rich men's houses. That must have been how she'd discovered this little secret passageway.

"How did you know about that?" the king demanded, and he was angry, clearly, but he'd also gone a little pale. So that she almost felt sorry for him.

"She remembered, obviously," Lysias replied for her, but he was also looking at her in a strange way. After a moment, he seemed to find himself and crossed to her. "You are overwhelmed," he said, and he sounded so kind and worried about her that she suddenly *was* overwhelmed.

"She remembers certain things, but others come back only in snatches," Lysias said to Diamandis, curling his arm around her waist in what felt like a protective gesture. "She needs some rest. Some quiet. I will take her back to—"

"You will take her upstairs. My staff has readied a room for her."

"Where she goes, I go. She is my fiancée, and I will not leave her alone to be tormented by the likes of you."

"If she really is my sister, an impossibility of course, I'd be saving her from the likes of *you*."

"Please," Al said, irritated with the both of them. "All this bitter fighting will get you nowhere. You both believe you are right and above reproach, and you'll never convince the other differently. So instead of bothering with all this male posturing, let us get to the heart of the matter."

Lysias smiled, but it was as fake as this little act. Still, he lifted her hand and brushed a kiss over the top of it, and no matter how off-kilter she felt, that was still a jolt of lust.

"Of course, *asteri mou*." He turned that sharp gaze to Diamandis. "Your Majesty, I did not expect you to believe me as a matter of course, but let us pursue civility." Lysias even smiled at his enemy. "We will get to the truth. *After* she has gotten some rest."

A muscle in Diamandis's jaw twitched, but he nodded. "We will indeed. Allow my staff to escort you to your rooms."

It was the king's turn to smile.

Lysias was not surprised exactly when it came to Alexandra's behavior in the king's study, though he didn't know how she'd figured out how to open the secret door. But she was the kind of woman who strode in and solved problems.

It was just so strange. This place. The cascade of emotions. *Her.* He had not prepared for this level of…upheaval.

This did not mean he was unequal to it, simply that he needed to center himself. Revenge required calculation and planning, and he was getting lost in pettiness that didn't matter. Not to his true goal.

But the hits kept coming. In the form of the cruel king. Because he recognized this back hallway. The more casual decor. No murals or gilded art. This was softer than the austere royal areas of the palace.

Because this was where the servants lived. Where *he* had lived. And when the guard, as if they really were prisoners, stopped in front of a door, Lysias's entire body went cold. The guard opened it and Alexandra stepped inside, but Lysias…

He should step inside. Freeze it out. Ignore this attempt at pain and suffering. He would prove to Diamandis that he could not be hurt. He *would*.

When he didn't follow, Alexandra looked back at him. Confusion and then concern clouding her features. "What's wrong?" she asked.

He should lie to her. Laugh it off. Something. But he could only find the means to tell her the truth. "These were my parents' quarters."

She blinked once, looked around the room. "That is cruel. That is…" She whirled, her expression an alluring mix of fire and her own revenge. She pushed passed him and the guard, striding down the hall back the way they'd come.

Both he and the guard were so surprised by her reaction, for a few moments they simply stood and stared after her.

But it was clear she wasn't going to come to her senses. Lysias strode after her before the guard could—making sure to block the guard's way so Lysias would be the first one to get to her.

"Alexandra."

She didn't so much as pause. She just kept walking quickly and certainly, retracing the exact path they'd just taken.

"Al."

But she did not stop, and he found himself so compelled by her anger, by *her* that he did not reach out and stop her, even though it would have been easy to do so.

The force of her. The way her skirts flowed behind her, like she was some sort of avenging Medusa. He wanted to see how this all went down.

She reached the office they'd just been in and threw the doors open with all the drama of a stage actress performing for a large crowd. The guard and Lysias followed her inside, where the king stood slowly from behind his desk, his expression a mix of such surprise and horror that Lysias had to bite back a laugh. Well, this was unexpected but rather enjoyable thus far.

Alexandra glowered up at Diamandis, hands fisted on her slim waist. "If you expect us to stay here, you will change our accommodations at once."

The king was silent for ticking seconds, but Alexandra did not back down. She held the king's gaze, her chest heaving in fury.

She truly was a beautiful little thing.

"If you were truly the lost princess of Kalyva, you would know better than to speak to your king in such a way," Diamandis said in a low, threatening tone.

Alexandra was clearly not intimidated. "I don't care if you are the king of the entire world." She flung her arms in the air, then pointed back to Lysias. "To put him in his parents' room, after the way he lost them, was a move of disgusting cruelty."

The king's face hardened more, if that were possible, and still Lysias could only watch in awe.

"But the two of you conspiring, lying, and you pretending to be my late sister is an act of charity?"

"So, an eye for an eye." She made a scoffing noise. "A king should be better, and I think we both know it's as possible that I am Zandra as anyone else. Whether you want to believe that or not, I do not care. What you have tried to do here is despicable. Perhaps I do not *wish* to be part of any royal family who would behave in such a way."

"The royal family, as you may have noticed, is dead."

"You are not."

Diamandis moved his gaze from Alexandra to Lysias. "You should control your fiancée," he said, drawing out the last word with disgust.

Lysias only smiled wider. "Oh, I much prefer her out of control. She is a thing of beauty, is she not?"

Diamandis looked Alexandra up and down. "I will enjoy proving you both to be the scheming, lying, charlatans that you are." He lifted his gaze to Lysias, who lounged quite comfortably against the wall. "So that there will be no question, Lysias, once and for all, that you are the same kind of traitor your parents were."

The words hit like the blow they were meant to be and reminded Lysias he was not here to watch Alexandra take Diamandis down a peg, no matter how much he enjoyed it. He could not be distracted in this way.

But when the guard showed them to a *new* room,

Lysias could not seem to find his old self. His singular focus on revenge.

For here was Alexandra, still angry and beautiful. And she'd faced down a king. His oldest enemy.

For him.

CHAPTER TEN

"I HATE HIM." Al seethed, pacing the new room. Oh, she'd gotten her way, but the anger hadn't receded. What a disgusting thing to do. Unforgivable. Lysias had looked so…

For the first time in that room in the servant's wing, she'd been able to picture the boy he might have been—the boy who'd allegedly been *friends* with the man who would torture him like this. The look on Lysias's face as he'd stood outside that room had cut her in two. And she'd felt honor bound to protect that hurt, abandoned, betrayed *boy*.

Lysias had said nothing as they'd been taken to their new quarters in a more elaborate part of the palace. Even *she* could tell the differences between the two areas, and that only made her angrier.

"I hate this *place*," Al said. Because she had so much anger twining with so much of that unsettled feeling, she simply needed to rage.

"I suppose both these things will only aid in my goal of revenge."

She turned to face Lysias, the odd note to his tone causing her some confusion. She thought perhaps he was trying to sound bored, but it did not come out with quite the same sarcasm he usually managed.

For the first time she considered that perhaps she should not have poked at the king like that. "Did I mess up your plans?" she asked. It struck her suddenly that she was not worried about upsetting his plans for the right reasons.

She didn't want him angry with her. She wanted him pleased. Approving. When she shouldn't care about *that*. She should care about enacting his revenge so she could get paid.

"No," Lysias replied, still hovering near the door, though he studied her with an intensity she could not fully understand, even if it made her heart begin to beat double time, and something improbably bloomed deep within.

"If anything," he continued. "I believe that little performance only adds credence to the belief we are devoted to one another. Which is good, as once it is proven you are the princess, a marriage to me will be his second-worst nightmare."

"But how can you prove…"

"I have worked for many years to get the people in the king's employ on my side. Some were glad to be the minute I approached…some took more time. Just this morning, I received confirmation that the palace doctor will falsify the DNA results for us."

Alexandra nodded, but his words did not bring

her comfort. He was staring at her a bit like they had never met, like he knew nothing about her and was surprised to find her here at all.

She didn't know what to say to him with that expression on his face. She did not know what the next step of any of this was. They were in the palace. They'd met with the king—who was as determined to prove them liars as Lysias had promised he would be.

He crossed to her then, and the look on his face sharpened, turning into something she might have called *feral*. There was something in his gaze—like last night, but not. He reached out and cupped her face with his large hands. He studied her for a moment more as her heart clattered about and her breath backed up in her lungs. As her body seemed to simply *come alight*.

And when he kissed her, it was not like yesterday. There was heat, yes. Passion. But something softer. Deeper. Whatever sharp-edged anger over Diamandis that had still been swirling inside of her settled, melted.

She leaned into him, into the kiss. She did not feel comfortable in this palace, and the only thing that seemed able to penetrate her unease was her anger.

And now this.

His hands smoothing over her back, large and possessive, drawing her closer against the hard evidence of his arousal. His mouth a dangerous demand of heat and something *more*.

When she managed to flutter her eyes open, his golden gaze was on her. Even as he kissed her rough and deep, he watched her. Lust bloomed suddenly, a bolt so hot and sharp it was nearly painful.

"Touch me," she managed, though her voice was ragged with that drugging need. She pressed herself against him, desperate for the way he could make her feel.

"You have forgotten the magic word, Alexandra," he said, his voice a deep purr. He'd stopped kissing her, and now he held her hips, his fingers curling in the fabric of her skirt that was held to the top with little fanciful ties of fabric.

She tried to move against him, find some satisfaction for herself, but he managed to hold her just out of reach. "Perhaps you should be the one saying please to me," she replied, looking for that balance they'd found last night. None of the disquiet she'd felt today.

He laughed darkly. "That will never happen." Then he ripped her skirt from the little ties in one hard jerk. She gasped at the arrow of pleasure that shot through her at such a reckless act. The skirt fluttered to the floor, but before she could even step out of it, he swept her into his arms and strode across the room to the bed—even larger than the one in his home.

He laid her down, straddling her body as he removed the top from her. She reached out and fumbled with the buttons of his shirt. She wanted to feel him. The heat of his skin, the power in his muscles.

He shrugged out of his shirt, then pulled her up by the shoulders to kiss her again, hard and deep. The tenor had changed from that first kiss, or so she thought. This one so fierce and wild and much more like last night.

Then he kissed down her neck, her chest, in between her breasts to where she still had a bandage. He brushed a light kiss over it. "Ah, *asteri mou*, no one will hurt you again. I will not allow it."

A warmth spread inside of her, along with all this passionate want. A strange moisture collected behind her eyes. It was a promise that he would not be able to keep, even if he meant to, because he would not be there once their little mission was finished. They would part. He had made that clear and she expected nothing more.

But he made her yearn for a more she had not imagined when she'd been Al and alone. She had never known anything of passion, but he had shown her last night. She had never known anything of whatever this was. She did not understand *this*. A tenderness that she had never seen in her life. A connection that felt beyond what physical sensations they could draw out in each other.

Like they were two sides of the same coin, melded together at last. *Belonging.* When she knew better than to belong to anyone or anything. The only permanence in life was oneself.

But his hand smoothed down her body, then cupped

her and the pleasure arrowed so deep, she was flying through her climax in mere moments. "Lysias…"

"More," he growled, and sheathed himself in protection before he thrust inside of her in one delicious slide. She moaned out his name, met each thrust with her own. She clung to him and chased every sensation wildly and wantonly, as he told her how beautiful she was, how *good*.

It never seemed to end, and she did not think her body could stand such pleasure, over and over, and yet the wave built. Larger and larger.

His hands tangled in her hair as he chased his release and she relished in the wild, uncontrolled beauty in it. In him. Her Lysias.

Finally. Finally. This was all she wanted. To be one with him. To ride this wave together. To forget all the world except him.

Except them.

And when he roared out his release, she didn't weep no matter how the tears built. She simply held on to him and did not let go.

She slept with her hand fisted at his heart, the ring on her finger sometimes catching the moonlight that slithered in through the curtains.

Lysias didn't sleep because a dark pain gripped him in its iron clutches. He knew if he slept, he would dream.

And he would dream of the monsters that even now he was trying to slay.

So he did not sleep. He lay in this foreign bed and felt the easy rise and fall of Alexandra's breathing.

Alexandra, *Al*, was a problem. She was perfection. The way she matched his passion for her. The way she had stood up *for* him. The whole of who she was…

She was a distraction he couldn't afford, and yet neither could he afford to set her aside. Her acting as his fiancée was an integral part of Lysias getting everything he wanted, of causing Diamandis the most amount of pain. He needed the princess she would play in order to take Diamandis out at the knees.

So something had to be done. He would need to be more careful. More guarded. He did not think resisting her was necessary per se. After all, that was simply…physical. Chemistry. A natural consequence to sharing so much time and space, and the beauty that she was.

He had simply not factored in that there would be an emotional response to returning to Kalyva. That seeing Diamandis would remind him of the time *before*. And while he had predicted many of Diamandis's moves, the king trying to put Lysias in his parents' old living quarters had been a cruelty he had not seen coming.

So he had learned his lesson. Expect pain and suffering and cruelty. Really, it was his life motto. It was ridiculous he'd been caught so off guard.

No matter. Diamandis would pay for it all.

Lysias couldn't forget himself just because his fake princess was...whatever she was. In the end, it did not matter. All that mattered was maintaining a certain wall of distance, of control.

It would be simple enough. There was much to do.

The king would demand a DNA test, and Lysias had to ensure all his men were in place to falsify the results. Something he had been working on for years, but even he could not have predicted the perfection that was Al. Without a past, there would be nothing to cast doubts on the falsified results.

But this was only a part of his plan. This was only a distraction. Perhaps it was even petty—much like Diamandis's attempt to put him in his parents' quarters. The main part of his plan was taking Diamandis's kingdom away from him.

For ten years, he had been finding not just people in the palace to betray Diamandis but people in the council, in Kalyva. It had taken time, subtlety, patience.

He finally had enough support to get a no-confidence vote. And Al—*Alexandra*—was the twist of the knife. While Diamandis was reeling over finding out his sister was alive, Lysias would tip the domino to ruin Diamandis's life.

He had *much* to do, and none of it included watching his fake fiancée begin to thrash in her sleep.

"The door," she muttered. "The door, the door." Then she began to cry quietly, and Lysias could feel her hot tears on his chest. "Am I safe here?"

Pain ripped through him, shadows creeping through the corners of his mind. *The door*. Someone else's voice. The cries and echoes of death. Of murder.

He squeezed his eyes shut, but that was worse. Images he'd long banished assaulted him. He opened his eyes again even as she thrashed more, cried harder.

He simply could not *bear* it. He gathered her close. Kissed her forehead. "Shh, *asteri mou*. You are always safe with me."

She let out a ragged breath, and the crying stopped. Slowly, she began to still. To breathe evenly once more. Without ever waking up.

Once she was calm, Lysias slid out of bed, surprised to find his hands were shaking. He curled them into fists and crossed to the window. He looked out into the night, where the stars and moon shone and rippled on the sea below. He took a deep breath, forced himself to settle.

All the ghosts and pain of his past existed on this little island, but once he took Diamandis's kingdom away from him, all would be well. All would be *soothed*.

He watched the sea as morning began its slow stretch toward dawn. Before the sun was fully up, he was dressed. He gave Alexandra one look. She was curled into a tight little ball, even as the sun made her skin glow gold.

No doubt she'd slept like that on the streets, and somehow she had survived. She was a marvel.

He dressed silently, then strode out of the bedroom and to the door that would lead him into the hall. He jerked the door open, something like panic trying to find some purchase inside of him. But he would not let it. He was in charge. He was Lysias Balaskas.

The guard stood there and Lysias scowled at him. "I wish to see the king."

The guard nodded, pointed down the hall. "He is waiting for you."

Of course he is. Lysias was led through the maze of the palace to Diamandis's office once more, though he knew the way himself. It was early, so the palace was even quieter than it had been yesterday. But there were guards stationed here and there in a way there had not been when the king and queen had been alive.

Lysias hoped it was because of him. He strode into the king's office and forced a smile. "Good morning, Your Majesty." Lysias greeted him with as much put-on cheer as he could muster—if only because it would serve to irritate the king. "My fiancée and I have much to accomplish today. I wish to show her the island, her birthright. Can I expect an armed guard tail as we do?"

Diamandis reacted to none of this. He simply sat at his desk and glowered. "I will see her alone."

Lysias had expected this, and still it was hard to keep his easy smile in place. "She will not want to see you without me. You may be surprised to find your welcoming demeanor yesterday did not win her over, and she is quite concerned about being here at all."

Diamandis looked at him with a raised brow. "Then leave."

Lysias tutted. "Now, no need to get all aflutter. Whatever you have to say to her, surely you can say in front of me. Her one true love."

"I don't know what you have done to this poor girl to make her believe there is an ounce of goodness in you, Lysias, or that she could possibly be a *princess*, but if you wish to remain, I will see her alone."

Lysias already knew he'd give in to Diamandis's wish. It was the only way, and he trusted Al to handle it beautifully. But he had to put up a fight for the show. "It is a blow, I know, to have your sister sullied by a *servant* such as me." He wasn't sure why *that* sentence felt so true when he was only playing a part. Only poking at Diamandis's weaknesses.

"A *traitor* such as you as long as you wear the last name Balaskas."

"You enjoy that word too much. Perhaps you need a lesson on its definition."

"You forget, Lysias, we had all the same lessons." Then Diamandis turned away, a cold dismissal. He began to walk out of the office, but he spoke as he did. "If she is not alone, I will not speak with her. And that will be that. I'll wait in the dining room."

Lysias said nothing, but he smiled at the king's retreating back. Because, yes, this was the plan.

When he returned to his rooms, Alexandra was

still in bed, though she was pushing herself into a sitting position as he entered the bedroom. Blinking at the light, holding the sheet lightly to her chest.

He wanted her with a powerful bolt of need, so much so he took a step forward. Ready to take and take and take until it was sated.

Then he remembered himself. He could enjoy her when the matters of the day were done, and they'd only just begun. "Ah, good morning, Alexandra. Best to be up and dressed." He strode through the room, keeping his gaze on anything but the tantalizing view of her beautiful frame.

He stopped at the window, looked out at the pretty, sunny beach below. He spoke to her without looking at her. "The king wishes to see you alone. I have, of course, put up a grand tantrum about the whole thing but eventually pretended to agree. You know your role, and while the king is busy with you, I will be able to ensure all the other puzzle pieces are in place."

"Lysias."

She said nothing else, and the silence stretched out until he forced himself to look at her with a self-satisfied expression. With the knowledge that revenge was within his grasp and nothing—*nothing*—else mattered.

There was some question in her dark gaze, some uncertainty in her expression. He did not know what she questioned, what worried her.

I do not want to know. Cannot know.

"Do you object to this plan?" he asked genially.

When she spoke, it was carefully, as if considering the question very seriously. "No, but—"

"Then dress, Alexandra. You have much to prove."

CHAPTER ELEVEN

ALEXANDRA GOT DRESSED. She supposed if she was breakfasting with a king, she should choose something elegant—not that any of the wardrobe Lysias, or rather his *team*, had supplied for her was anything other than elegant—but she didn't want to wear a gown or heels. She knew she *should* dress the part of the princess, but she just felt…exhausted. Oddly wrung out.

And yes, some of that was the way she felt in this place, but most of it was Lysias. The feelings he was pulling out of her. She didn't understand them—so new, so foreign, but she knew they were dangerous, and if anyone suffered from them, it would be herself.

She sighed and found some trousers, though they were flowy and silk and not like the kind she'd worn when she'd pretended to be a boy. She paired these with a matching shirt and then studied herself in the mirror. Even without doing her hair or makeup, she looked like a woman. It was quite a marvel what the right cut of clothes could accomplish.

But because she enjoyed it, and it added a regal air to the whole facade, she sat down and did her hair and makeup just as Lysias's staff had taught her. A few days' practice was hardly enough to make her an expert, but she managed well enough.

Then she studied her face, her profile, then straight on. *Did* she look like Diamandis? Maybe something in the way their eyes were situated on their face. And the color, sure, but many people had dark brown eyes. *Obviously*, they weren't actually related, but clearly, Diamandis had not fully refused the possibility out of hand.

When she returned to the main room of their quarters, she found them empty. And simply stood for odd moments of… What was this feeling? It camped out in her chest and moved into her throat. As if she might cry.

Which she would *not* do.

She sucked in a breath and focused. She was to face King Diamandis alone. She had thought Lysias would be with her at least until they got to the dining room, but no matter. She often worked alone. She *always* worked alone. It would be better. She could handle this how she saw fit.

Without worrying so much for Lysias's approval.

She frowned at the voice in her head speaking truths she did not wish to acknowledge. Poking at feelings so deep and foreign and new, the thought of parsing through them was…terrifying.

So she straightened her shoulders and marched out into the hall. A guard stood there and bowed when she emerged.

"Miss. The king wishes for you to join him for breakfast. I will accompany you to the dining room."

Alexandra smiled *prettily* at him, just as Lysias had taught her to. "That would be wonderful. Thank you."

The guard led her through the palace. It was a long walk to the dining room. "Why are there so many armed men within the palace?" Al asked, as much out of curiosity as anything. No doubt Lysias already knew the answer, but she hadn't thought to ask him yet.

"We protect the king."

"Yes, but couldn't you protect him outside? Isn't it usually some kind of…butler or some such that leads prisoners—oh, *dear*, I mean guests—about the palace?" She smiled at the guard and watched the expression on his face, but it did not change at the word "prisoner." Either he thought she was being foolish enough to ignore, or he was just comfortable with her actually being a prisoner. Al supposed it didn't matter which one.

"We protect the king," he repeated, rather robotically. He led her to yet another huge pair of double doors and opened them before pointing her inside.

It was a huge room, with a long, long table at the

center. At the very end sat the king. Al knew she
should forget about being put in Lysias's parents'
quarters yesterday, but she found she could not. Nor
could she ignore the fact this man had exiled Lysias
at the age of *twelve*. Even if he'd been only a few
years older himself.

Clearly, King Diamandis *was* the villain Lysias
made him out to be, and so she would win this little
round of make believe. For Lysias.

Because he had called her an avenger, and she
would avenge the little boy he'd been. Treated so
cruelly by this *king*.

Do you really think that will make him love you?

Love. What had she ever known of love? Nothing.
So it was foolish to think on it at all. She was savvy
enough to know that sex did not equal love, even if
she'd never engaged in the act before.

Men were pigs, after all. The one sitting at the
table inspecting her like a bug was chief among
them.

"Shall I sit down here so we can shout across the
room to each other?" Al called out, smiling a bit at
the way her voice echoed in the large room.

Though it was quite a way down the line, she saw
the king startle a bit. Clearly not expecting her voice
to boom across the tall, grand arched ceilings.

"There is a seat for you down here," Diamandis replied, and while his voice was commanding, it
didn't seem to echo quite the way hers had.

So, Al made her way down the long table, taking

in everything. The richness of the wood, the way the art in here depicted feasts of days gone by. The soaring windows with their beautiful views out to the sea.

When Al finally found the place that had clearly been laid out for her, she made sure to lower herself as gracefully as possible into the plush seat. She fixed the sweetest smile on her face. "Good morning, Your Majesty."

The king's eyes narrowed. "What is he promising you?"

"No pleasantries, then? Ah, very well. I believe he's promising me a lifetime of commitment," Al replied blandly. She lifted her engagement ring and allowed it to sparkle in the light streaming in through the window before she studied the spread before her. Platters of food—pastries, breakfast meats, yogurts and such were laid out with little tongs. There were also pitchers of juice, a pot of coffee. Such choices. She supposed it paid to be the king.

"May I?" she asked.

The king's expression became more and more thunderous, which Al could admit brought her some petty joy. She didn't wait for his permission. She poured herself some coffee from the ornate pot. She helped herself to a little of everything laid before her and vowed then and there that no matter how much money she had after her payout, she would always be grateful for food without worry.

"You will be found out. I am a *king*. I realize our country is small and not well known. That many in the outside world consider us so old-fashioned that we have no power, but I have the power to find the truth about you. And destroy you."

Al did not laugh, though a strange bubble of it rose inside her chest. "I suppose it's handy then that there's nothing to destroy."

"You sound like him," Diamandis muttered disgustedly.

"We are quite alike, my beloved and I." *Beloved* landed a bit clunkily, but Al did not look at Diamandis when she said it. She pretended to be so engaged in her eating she couldn't possibly look up.

"I will destroy you both."

Al sighed heavily and leaned her chin on her hand before studying the man who was king of this pretty little island. There was no doubt in her mind he didn't deserve the power, the position. "Do you men ever get tired of wanting to destroy things?"

Diamandis pushed back from the table, tossing his napkin down on his plate. "I have work to do. To find the truth. Feel free to pass that along to Lysias."

"Oh, I don't need to. I think you must underestimate him. Do you really believe he'd bring me here without having thought of everything?" She looked up at the King, wholly unbothered by his bluster.

Because underneath, she saw something that reminded her of fear. Not of Lysias or his revenge, she didn't think. But fear that it could be true. That she might actually be Princess Zandra.

Which meant they'd never found a body, if he could worry about *truths*.

He leaned in close, all thunderstorms and rage. "Tell me one thing," he demanded, eyes blazing. Eyes like her own. "One thing only Zandra Agonas would know."

If he was questioning her, it meant he thought it was possible she was Zandra. She didn't let her triumph at that show, because his face was too close. She could *feel* the hot anger radiating off him. And she had the strangest impulse to reach out and…poke him right in the middle of his Adam's apple.

She didn't even stop herself. She just did it. *Poke.*

He stumbled back, his hand flying to his throat. She frowned a little, because while it had no doubt felt uncomfortable, she'd hardly *punched* him there. It shouldn't have hurt *that* much.

But he'd paled, his hand on his throat like she'd stabbed him clean through. "That proves nothing," he said raggedly, stepping away from her as if she were suddenly venomous.

Which was an odd thing to say since she didn't know what poking him was meant to prove. She'd only done it out of impulse, out of frustration. Perhaps he just wasn't used to people not being afraid of him. He seemed the kind of king who dealt in fear.

Then he strode out of the dining room, and since Alexandra had nothing else to do, she gorged herself on breakfast.

* * *

Lysias returned to the palace in a good mood. Though he'd known the guards had followed him, he'd also lost them here and there to do what needed to be done before allowing them to catch up to him once more.

They would report to Diamandis that they had lost him for pieces of time, and Diamandis would, of course, find this suspicious, but even if he found out what Lysias was doing, he wouldn't be able to stop it.

It was a decade in the making. At first, Lysias had bribed people because he'd been new to money and power. But as the decade had gone on, as he'd grown in that money and power, he'd begun to understand people better. Kalyva better. And the way Diamandis ruled more clearly.

So over the years, he'd learned to prey on people's sense of injustices done against them. Though Diamandis treated most of his staff well, according to what Lysias heard, the man was hard on people who disagreed with him or who failed.

So, Lysias had begun to target those men. Sway them to his side. And let the spiderwebs of discontent spread out until the perfect moment.

That was the beauty of public opinion. Because everything was set up perfectly. When Diamandis presided over the council meeting next week, there would be a vote of no confidence. It paid to know the laws of Kalyva, and that while the monarchy ruled exclusively, the council had the right to run checks and balances.

One of the rarely used balances was a vote of no confidence against the king, and if popular vote of the council resulted in no confidence, it could choose a new king. Lysias had considered himself for the position but wasn't sure he wanted to deal in the politics of it all.

Then there was Al, but she would need to make herself scarce in case the truth every came out.

So, some stranger would take over Kalyva, and for Diamandis, that would be failure enough.

Lysias smiled. Much could still go wrong, but he simply wouldn't allow it. He was too close and had come too far.

So he strode through the palace, knowing he was being watched but was thrilled with the successes he'd made today. He also told himself over and over again as the anticipation rose within him that this feeling was all about the future success of his plan.

Not returning to his Alexandra.

He opened the door to the main room and ignored the jolt of worry and frustration that twined within him when she clearly wasn't there. He moved through the bedroom, the dressing rooms, then back out to the bedroom with increasing frustration.

When he finally caught a glimpse of her, it was through the large-windowed door that led out to a little balcony. She stood out on it, leaned over the rail, her hair blowing gently in the slight breeze. She wore pants today, but the material looked like silk and billowed in the breeze like her hair.

He simply stopped and watched. Her eyes were on the blazing sunset meeting the darkening sea. It was hard to believe he'd ever taken her for a boy. She was so beautiful. Alluring and self-possessed with a curiosity for life that he'd never seen matched. She'd attempted to protect him, *avenge* him, when no one had since he'd been a boy.

And when she touched him, kissed him, came apart around him, he was transported to another world entirely. One where revenge didn't matter at all.

He was desperate for her, and he didn't understand. Had she cast a spell on him? Poisoned him? Because he wanted her naked and beneath him, but he also wanted to stand here and watch her for eternity.

It was the thought of *eternity* that had him moving forward, breaking this little moment of insanity, because he needed to know how her breakfast had gone, and keep her abreast of her next steps.

Because revenge was all that truly mattered here in Kalyva.

She looked over her shoulder at him, and everything in her expression lightened. She smiled as if she were happy to see him. As if she'd been waiting for him.

An echoing warmth bloomed within him, and it reminded him of his childhood here. Of that feeling of belonging, being so sure of his place. It had not mattered that he was a servant. There'd been little struggle. So much freedom.

And love.

And then everyone he loved had been murdered. Had betrayed him. How dare she bring that out in him again. Muddle all his revenge with this...this... *feeling*.

But she seemed clueless to the storm within him. "Were you successful?" she asked pleasantly.

He worked very hard to chain down his volatile emotions. To speak as pleasantly in return as she spoke to him. "Very. Everything is in place. We will agree to the DNA test the next time Diamandis presses the issue, and my men will ensure the results show a match with Diamandis. Did you do any work as AI today?"

Some of her smile dimmed at this, and she began to worry her bottom lip between her teeth. She looked back at the sea. "No. My meeting with the king was very short, but I think... There is no body," she said, almost thoughtfully. "The king asked me to prove I was Zandra. I guess it could all be his own game, but he seemed..." She paused as if searching for the right word. "I think he's afraid I *could* be her, which means he knows that no body was ever found, doesn't it? He seemed so genuinely angry, demanding I prove myself. I just don't see how there is a body anyone knows of."

Lysias wasn't sure why he was surprised. He'd

suspected this ever since Diamandis brought them to the palace. There was simply no reason if he was *certain* Zandra was dead. And still, it shocked him a bit to hear Alexandra confirm it because he'd still been suspicious of Diamandis playing a game.

"What did you mean at the beach yesterday?" she asked, turning her attention back to him. "When you said you knew she wasn't with her siblings because you were there?"

He was already feeling volatile, nearly unhinged with a million battering emotions. Remembering that night would break the chain of his control. So he tried not to *remember*, only to repeat basic facts.

"I was in the palace that night," he responded, as if by rote. "I knew Zandra was not with her siblings. She was in her own nursery. She might have been killed, but not with them." It was not the full truth, but it was the only truth he wanted to live in.

Alexandra nodded thoughtfully. "Do you think I could be from here?" she asked, pointing down at the village below.

"What do you mean?"

"I don't really remember my life before Athens. Maybe I didn't have one. But something about this place is so familiar and uncomfortable. If there was the upheaval of a coup or what have you, maybe I was here. Maybe that's the source of my nightmares." Her gaze moved from the sea to him. "Do you think it possible?"

With her, anything seemed possible. And since he

knew firsthand the pain and suffering of that night, he would not put it past anyone to have nightmares and to have forgotten. Especially since she wouldn't have been more than four herself.

He reached out, though he knew he shouldn't, ran his hand over the silk of her hair. The way it burned with hints of red as the sun disappeared behind him. "I am falsifying the DNA results for the king, of course, but if you wish, I could run a real test. Anonymously. See if you match anyone. It is not a surety, as any relative would have to be in a system we run it through. But…it would be a chance."

She stood very still, staring at him with wide eyes. "Really?"

"Of course," he said roughly.

She leaned forward, reaching out to put her hands on his chest. Over his heart. She was searching his face. "Lysias…"

He saw something in her eyes, something soft. Dangerous. And he shook his head. He would not allow it. He would cut this off at the pass. "I have been clear, Alexandra," he said stiffly.

"Yes. You've been clear," she agreed. Easily and with no hint of hurt, but that only made him unreasonably angry. That she'd leave her hands over his heart. That she'd look up at him as if she understood him when he hadn't even explained.

When no one could understand.

But she thought she did. He saw it there in the way she looked at him. She thought she saw *him*, and he had to prove to her that she was wrong. It was a raging anger inside of him.

He curled his hand in her hair, used it as leverage to tip her head back, so she met his gaze head on. And she didn't look away, didn't struggle. She simply looked up at him. So calm. So sure.

"Everyone I have ever loved has died brutally or betrayed me," he told her. Because she *would* understand. If he had to bellow it from the mountaintops. "I will never shackle myself to another. I will never let anyone have power over me again. I am the only power."

"Yes," she agreed, so readily. So *calmly*, not even trying to pull her hair from his grasp. "Except you want me," she said, reaching out to trace the evidence of this fact, without ever taking her gaze from his eyes.

"This is *all* I want from you," he growled.

"Then take it, Lysias."

Was it challenge? Was it surrender? He didn't know. He didn't care. He took her mouth with his in angry demand. Fisted his hands in her hair to hold her still while he took what *he* wanted. What *he* desired.

But she met him there, in this fiery insanity between them. Where all rational thought burned away into only their bodies. He ripped her trousers away from her, even as she worked his belt free.

He didn't bother with her shirt, didn't want to see the evidence of where she'd been injured. Didn't want to believe her capable of being hurt. He backed her against the wall, so that she stepped out of her pants and underwear.

The breeze rippled through his hair, and he didn't care they were outside. All he cared about was possession. The deep, dark thing that beat within him, twining with the anger and the other emotion he refused to acknowledge. But it gave everything claws. Teeth.

He pulled her leg up to wrap around his waist but held her there so he could look at her. Where she was wet for him. His gaze raked up to meet hers.

She breathed heavily, but she only looked at him. With softness in her gaze, even as he was rough with her.

"You want me like this?" He could see that she did, *feel* that she did. And yet he wanted to hear her say it. As if that would give him permission to take whatever he wanted, however he wanted.

"Yes. There isn't a way I don't want you," she said, and it didn't sound soft, it sounded strong. Like she was the one in control.

Never. How dare she sound so calm. So perfectly *rational* when he wanted to rage against everything that swirled inside of him. Everything she brought out in him. Everything he'd buried so deep it lived with the shadows and monsters of his nightmares.

So he took her. Her back against the wall, her legs wrapped around him as he plunged. He gave her no quarter, no rest. And she didn't ask for any. Simply begged for more, shattering over and over again. Her nails dug into his back. She set her teeth to his neck. She said his name, sobbed it. As night fell over them.

But it did not matter how rough he was with her, how much he'd hoped to drive some wedge between what they were and the feelings she'd unwisely left clear in her eyes.

Even as he carried her inside, bent her over the bed and slid into her from behind. Even as he made her say *please* over and over again, until he finally roared out his release, his fingers digging into her slim hips.

Even with all that, when all was said and done, she still curled up next to him and fell into a quiet sleep.

With her hand fisted over his heart as if she held it there.

CHAPTER TWELVE

ALEXANDRA WASN'T SURPRISED to wake up alone. Even though she knew Lysias had stayed with her for a portion of the evening, it seemed impossible to think he'd actually face the aftermath in the waking hours if he'd only faced them with sex the night before.

She sighed and looked up at the ceiling. She didn't know what he thought he'd been doing last night. Driving her away from him? Proving some point about emotions? All he'd managed to do was strip away everything until she couldn't deny one simple truth.

She loved him.

What a strange series of events. She knew that it was foolish for a girl such as her to think she knew anything of love, that love could bloom in a matter of days, but... She just did. She wished to help him, to avenge him. She wanted to spend time with him—inside and outside of their bed.

The Lysias who forgot about his revenge was a caretaker, as if he couldn't help himself. An avenger too. She'd seen an Athenian paper yesterday in the sitting room with a pile of newspapers from all over. On the front page had been a picture of Vasilis Pangali in handcuffs.

The man who'd sent her attacker. She *knew* Lysias was behind it—because no one else could possibly be.

And yet she knew Lysias did not fancy his moral code above anyone else's. She loved him because she understood him. Everything he must have endured to rise to the top and still remain cognizant of the lows he'd come from. He was wholly himself and not afraid to enact what he believed in.

Except when it came to love.

She thought, perhaps foolishly, that he might love her too if he could get past the fear that held him in its grips—that he hid with fake masks and revenge plots.

It seemed a rather big if, considering that fear had clearly driven his need for revenge across two decades. That his fear lived deep within an old trauma he could not seem to face.

She rolled onto her stomach, surveyed the world outside the large windows and doors that led to the balcony. The sun had begun its rise, but it was still early yet, so the world glowed a dim gold as the sea moved in the distance.

She had no doubt Lysias was out enacting plots and plans. She likely wouldn't see him again until evening. Like last night.

She thought of last night. Of the rough way he'd taken her, out on the balcony and then on this bed. She was getting warm and excited just thinking about it.

She had reveled in the wildness because she understood it. She understood *him*. Something as soft and dangerous as love felt like a loss of control. Like a threat. He'd needed to fight that threat.

And the fight had been glorious. They had left marks on each other, yes, but they had climbed to new heights of pleasure. And maybe he had not come to the same conclusion she had—that loving him was simply an inescapable fact of life, no matter how vulnerable it made her—but it had burned away some of the fear. For her.

Growing up as she had, accepting things became necessary, whether they were comfortable or not. If she denied simple truths, she would end up in danger or worse. So she simply had to accept that she'd fallen in love with him.

If it hurt, if it ended, that would be terrible, yes, but life was oftentimes terrible, and she would simply move through the terrible as she'd done so many times before.

For whatever reason, Lysias did not have that skill. He was stuck in the tragedy of his past. Maybe… She hoped so much that dealing with all of this revenge would make him more open to the idea, the possibility.

But if it didn't, she would survive. She was certain she would be able to survive. Had to be.

Lysias would as well, survivor that he was, but she wanted to give him more than survival. Which would require being careful with him, with her feelings.

How would he behave this evening?

Would he pretend nothing had happened? Try to be cruel to her now? Maybe they would repeat the intensity of last night. Or maybe…maybe he would send her away.

The first trickle of fear slithered around her heart. She could handle it all—she could pretend with the best of them, and she could weather his cruelty. She reveled in his demands, but she could not be sent away. She *needed* to be by his side. Especially as he took on the king.

The king who clearly thought Alexandra *could* be his long-lost sister. She didn't know how she felt about that. In preparation for this time on Kalyva, it had only been about *her*. That she could play the role that had been designed for *her*. She hadn't thought about *him*. About Diamandis.

Now she'd come face-to-face with him, so she had no choice but to regard him as a human being. Even though she rather detested that person, it was cruel what they were doing. To make him believe his sister was alive and here.

She blew out a frustrated breath and crawled out of bed. Naked, she padded over to her wardrobe. She considered dressing as Al, sneaking about the palace as a boy, but when faced with her closet, she reached for a colorful sun dress instead.

She might be forced to return to Al yet. Why not enjoy Alexandra while she could?

So she dressed, she curled her hair and took time on her makeup. She studied herself, as it seemed she was incapable of passing a mirror without looking for the similarities between her and the king that would make anyone consider the possibility they were related.

Did they have similar ears? Was their chin pointed in the same way?

She shook her head and looked away. She never found answers, and it was a pointless endeavor anyway, as she was not his sister.

When she stepped out of the rooms, the guard was waiting for her in the hall as always. She smiled pleasantly at him, even though she was tired of being followed and led about. "Oh, would the king like me to breakfast with him again?" she asked, making sure to sound sugary sweet. "Or are you just today's chosen jailor?"

"I will take you to the dining room, miss," he said. Not answering her questions at all.

She let the guard guide her to breakfast, but she'd been watching them. And taking note of the different areas in the palace that were guarded and not. The dining room was empty, save a place set for her, so she sat down and ate another delicious, filling breakfast.

All the while, she watched the guard by the door out of the corner of her eye. When he was busy flirting with one of the kitchen staff, Alexandra slid silently out of the room through the hallway that led around the kitchen and into another wing of the palace.

She stood in the hallway listening for guards or people but heard nothing except an oppressive kind of silence. A velvet rope hung at the end of the staircase at the end of the hall. Like they were in some sort of museum, and this section was not allowed visitors.

Naturally, she couldn't resist. She stepped over the rope, then took the stairs. The carpet was so plush she didn't even need to try to soften her footfalls.

Something whispered through her, over her skin as she took each stair. A kind of foreboding, and yet a curiosity so deep she couldn't resist.

She let those odd whispers guide her up the ornate staircase, pausing to gaze out the large windows that lined the walls along the way. She took in all that sea that surrounded so much of the palace. No matter how it made her feel, it was a truly beautiful place.

The staircase spiraled up and around until she was at the top and greeted with another long, grand hallway. There was a huge painting at the end of it. Alexandra moved for it. A cover hung from the bottom edge, like someone had recently pulled it off.

When she approached, she stared up at the portrait of a couple in grand royal garb, down to crowns and scepters. They were both smiling. The man looked so much like Diamandis she almost thought it *was* him, but the woman...

In the woman's face, she found a startling resemblance. Not identical. In fact, she might not have noticed at all if she hadn't spent the past few days studying her own face, comparing it to Diamandis's. But this woman's cheeks moved into her nose in the same delicate fashion Al had always tried to hide when living as a boy. The sweep of this woman's hair revealed ears and a dainty jawline that just... felt familiar.

And her eyes, even just in the painting, radiated a warmth that made Alexandra struggle to breathe.

A dark, cold fear took hold of her, and she had to look away, or she might burst into tears she did not understand.

She was faced with a row of doors as she fought the emotional outpouring. All were closed. Except one, which was opened a crack.

Compelled, Alexandra moved forward. With all the stealth of her spy days, she eased the door open a little bit at a time. It was a room. Maybe a bedroom? But it was hard to tell as most of the furniture and belongings were covered. Except a few things had clearly been disturbed recently.

And someone was in here. She could hear their audible breaths, though she would need to open the door wider to see who it was.

It didn't matter who it might be. She should leave. She had no business being here.

But she didn't leave. She pushed the door open wider until she could see a man. Gazing out a high window—the only source of light in the entire dark room. The shafts of light danced with dust motes and haloed him standing there.

"Lysias," she breathed.

He stilled—the only sign she might have startled him. Then slowly he turned to face her, his expression utterly blank.

"Were you followed?" he asked.

"Of course not," she replied. Luckily, the question offended her enough that she wasn't shaky when she spoke. "No one can guard me for long. What about you?"

He turned to look back out the window. Unlike most of the other windows in the house that she'd seen, it did not go to the floor. It started above Lysias's tall frame and reached to the high ceiling. "I know the palace too well not to be able to slip away as it suits me."

"No doubt they'll find us soon enough with the way guards roam this place," Al said, carefully taking steps to come closer to him. But not too close. Part of her was afraid if she got too close, he'd be cold or cruel or make them both leave.

"He is paranoid of his own bloody coup." Lysias shrugged. "Which is fair."

So they were to ignore last night. Ignore their feelings. Alexandra found she was okay with that for the time being because this room gave her a disquieted feeling in the pit of her stomach, and yet she could not find the sense to want to leave.

"What room is this?" she asked, studying what she could make out of it in the dim light. Though many things were covered, the walls were visible and beautiful. Painted with bright, vibrant scenes that looked like something out of a fairy tale. Princesses in the forests and fairies flitting about trees.

"A nursery," Lysias said after a beat of hesitation.

"Who's nursery?" Alexandra replied, smiling as she reached out to touch the outline of a glistening dragon painted gliding above the trees.

He sighed. Heavily. "The princess."

Alexandra jerked her hand back as if she'd been burned. It felt wrong, she did not know why. She turned to Lysias, though he still simply stood there, hands clasped behind his back, staring out the window. "Why are you in here?" she asked, desperate for him to give her an honest answer.

Because *this* didn't seem to be about revenge. There was something...sadder at play here.

He didn't answer or react right away. Almost as if she weren't here at all. "I did not mean to be," he said after a while. Which broke her heart.

She crossed to him, needing to comfort him whether he would accept that comfort or not. He sounded so pained. Looked so lost. She slid her hand up his back. She opened her mouth to speak, but the scene below the high window caught her eye. It depicted a very thick tree trunk, little, colorful birds dancing around it.

But it wasn't a tree, she knew. Much like the art panel in Diamandis's office. This was something else.

Another door. She could see the outline of it in the dark paint of the tree trunk.

"Lysias," she whispered, because she felt a very real fear even though she was in no danger.

"What?"

She pointed at the tree. "This is the door. The door in my dream."

Lysias didn't speak. He could not find the words. He wanted to call her a liar, but he saw the way she looked at the tree, where there was indeed a door.

He'd *heard her* mutter about the door in her sleep. Say something he'd once heard someone else say. When he'd set her inside that door.

Am I safe here?

The clawing at his chest he couldn't eradicate squeezed at his lungs. Memories, yes, but something more. Something to do with Alexandra.

Who crouched down, reached out, and touched the exact spot on the tree that popped the door open.

He saw her in profile, and it melded with a flash of the queen. A kind woman. Whose profile looked so like Alexandra's. He'd pushed those memories out of his mind. Blackened them in shadow. Until he'd found himself compelled to walk up here and come face-to-face with the dusty portraits of the king and queen he remembered.

But it couldn't *be*.

Alexandra looked up at him, tears in her eyes. "What happened here?" she asked.

And he knew he shouldn't tell her. That whatever this was, it wasn't about the events in this room. It wasn't about… Alexandra. No matter what strange parts of the palace she knew.

But the images were there, dancing around, and it seemed he had to speak them into existence or be haunted forever. How would he enact his revenge if he could not deal in hard truths?

"This was Princess Zandra's nursery, as I said. Diamandis's room was at the beginning of the hall, as he was a teenager and the heir. The two middle boys, they had their own rooms on the opposite side of the hall, but they were twins. So similar, they were an inseparable duo. No matter how their nannies or parents tried, they always ended up together in one room. Wreaking havoc. Zandra was the only girl and much younger, so this was hers."

Alexandra stayed crouched there, but then she opened the door wider. Without thinking it through, an impulse born of sheer terror, his hand reached out and grabbed her roughly away.

But she looked up at him, even as he held her elbow. "Lysias, what *happened*?"

"On that night… I was with my parents, in our

quarters, when we first heard the screams. Gunfire. People fled, crying that the king and queen had been murdered. My parents… They put me in the tunnel to keep me safe. The tunnels, they are old. From early denizens of the palace. By the time I was a child, they were simply used as a playhouse for the children. Including me. So my parents thought I would be safe there."

"Were you?" she asked, breathlessly. As if he wasn't standing before her, alive and well.

"I was, but I knew… I knew the men who'd killed the king and queen would go after the children."

It all came flooding back. Everything he'd blocked out for so long. The gunfire, the screams, his parents' wild eyes as they'd huddled in their rooms, praying the rebellious group would not come for the servants.

Their desperation to save him when it seemed they would.

He'd known the memories would attack him if he came up here, but he hadn't been able to resist. Maybe he'd had some foolish belief he could stare it down and forget it forever. Instead he was reliving it, holding Alexandra there at arm's length.

And it poured out of him. How he had paused there in the tunnels, wondering what he should do. That it had been the thought of his best friend being killed that he could not stand. So he'd made his way through the maze that would lead him to Diamandis's room. But he searched the room, and Diamandis wasn't there.

"I thought perhaps he'd gone to save the others,

so I looked out of his door. There were men break-ing into the room across the hall, where I knew the twins were. Shooting. The screams…"

Maybe she said something, but he didn't hear it. He was too lost in that old nightmare.

"But I thought if the gunmen were there, they hadn't gotten to the princess yet. And maybe Dia-mandis was with Zandra. I could not save the boys, but maybe I could save them. So I went back to the tunnels, came out here." He pointed to the door she'd opened.

"Diamandis was not here, but Zandra was. She was sitting in her bed. I told her she had to come to the tunnels, to be safe. She didn't respond. I don't know what she'd seen or hadn't, but when I finally went over to her bed, she got out and took my hand. I took Zandra through the door. I told her we would go to my parents. My parents never would have harmed a child. *Never.*"

"You saved her," Alexandra whispered, and there was awe in her tone. Misplaced awe though it was.

"I tried. I do not know what became of her." *Will I be safe here?* But he had never had time to answer. "I could hear them coming, so I shoved her into the wall and closed the door before the men burst into the room. They said something to each other about me being a servant, not what they were after. I do not know what they did to me, only that it rendered me unconscious. When I woke up, bloody and hurt-ing, I was in a prison. Alone. I was never allowed to speak to my parents again. They were taken away and executed the following day."

"Lysias…"

"I don't know what saved me from the same fate. My age. My friendship with Diamandis. They said the princess was dead, and I believed them, but I knew my parents had nothing to do with it. Maybe she took the wrong tunnel. Maybe the men found her. I will never know, but I know my parents did not kill her, and they did not deserve to be executed."

She nodded, swallowing convulsively. "I believe you," she said.

All the old monsters roared in some kind of pained relief. For no one, not one person since that night ever had. He felt torn apart, flayed open. A wounded animal with no recourse but to lash out.

Except his Alexandra was all color and light, standing there with teardrops on her cheeks. Brown eyes wide and sympathetic.

"If you do not know what became of her…" Alexandra looked down at the door, and he knew she was considering the impossible idea that had been trying to take root in his mind since she had opened the door in Diamandis's office.

"It couldn't be true, Alexandra," he said harshly. Because maybe some strange part of him *wanted* it to be. "It couldn't be possibly true."

"No, of course not." She looked up at him and smiled, but there was a sadness in her eyes that carved him up inside. "Perhaps I was like you. A servant here. That would explain things, would it not?"

He doubted it very much, as he couldn't think of any servant children young enough to be her, but still he nodded, because it was better than the alternative.

The impossible.

"Perhaps."

"I doubt very much we will ever know, as it seems unlikely my true family would be in some DNA database, and it truly is of no matter. Your parents were wronged, and we will find a way to right that wrong. Together."

There had not been anyone on his side since he was twelve. But he did not want her here. He wanted to do this alone. To prove to Diamandis that nothing, *nothing* could touch the man he'd made himself into.

He meant to tell her that. To chastise her for butting her nose into his business when she was a tool. Nothing more. But the words did not come out, and he heard the squeak of the door, the sound of new footsteps.

He turned, reflexively keeping Alexandra behind him in a move of protection. He scowled at Diamandis, who stood just outside the door with his own deep scowl.

"What are you two plotting?" he asked darkly. "*My* death this time around?"

CHAPTER THIRTEEN

ALEXANDRA WAS MORE shaken than she could remember being. Except maybe when her attacker had caught up to her back in Athens.

But this was not an attack. It was just…sad.

And strange. She glanced back at the tree door. How had she known? Why did this palace awaken such strange things inside of her?

But she could not worry over it now. They needed to face down Diamandis. As a united front.

Alexandra hooked her arm through Lysias's. She smiled sadly at Diamandis and used all the truths that made even her wonder why she felt connected to this place. "I suffer nightmares. Of a door. When I explained the door in my dreams to Lysias, he brought me up here."

Diamandis sighed disgustedly. "You mean he brought you up here to fill your head with lies?"

"No, I do not mean that," she replied, firmly, as if she were speaking to a child.

"I know your game, Lysias. You've told her your

own memories so she can pretend they are her own." Then, surprisingly, his gaze turned toward her. "You think you can poke me in the throat and convince me of this ridiculous charade? I am not so easily swayed. My private doctor is here ready to administer the DNA swab. Let's get this over with."

Lysias did not move forward. He looked down at her like Diamandis had accused her of speaking in tongues. "You...poked him?" Lysias said, sounding oddly ragged. "In the *throat*?"

"I realize he's a king and all, but he was in my face. I don't understand the big deal." But clearly it was some kind of...deal.

"Where will she be given the swab?" Lysias asked, returning his gaze to Diamandis, his tone back to being detached and firm.

"In my office."

"We will meet you there in a moment."

"You think I'd leave you here alone? That I'd let you continue to desecrate my sister's memory?"

Lysias laughed darkly. "You care for her memory? As I recall, you were nowhere to be found that night." They moved toward each other, two angry men seething with all their old hurts and tragedies dressed up like fury.

But they were both just...injured, traumatized boys, Alexandra realized.

She stepped in between them before they could land the blows they both clearly wanted to. Their anger tied her stomach in knots, though she couldn't

quite work out why. They were enemies, but it felt
wrong that they should fight. Here of all places.

"Come, Diamandis. I'll let you take your little
swab," she said, with a wave toward the door.

He sneered at her. "You'll not order me around,
imposter."

"I suppose I understand why you feel the need to
rage and threaten us, but the fact of the matter is you
haven't tossed us out yet. So you know it's possible
I might be your sister. If you feel better to treat me
so shabbily because you think there's a chance I'm
not, very well. But I find it tiring."

She surveyed them both, decided to take the role
of cool, regal *princess*. She wasn't, of course she
wasn't. No matter what strange snatches of memory
seemed to exist here. But that was the role she'd been
brought here to play.

"If you must have a bit of manly fistfighting to
make yourselves feel better, you should take it outside. And leave me out of it." And with that, Alexandra left the room with its echoes of pain and violence.
The strange tree door from her dreams.

She wanted this over now more than ever. But
then, she would not have Lysias, and that was a new
pain. To think of life without him.

She had to push away that thought. She couldn't
make him love her. Or be brave enough to love
her. Maybe she didn't need to. Maybe she could
simply convince him that since they got along so

well, they should continue to enjoy each other... until they didn't.

Somewhat relieved by this plan, she walked back down the staircase. The men followed, though a few paces back.

Alexandra didn't look around this time. She ignored the whispers and shadows. She wanted no memories. No snatches of this possibility that *she* was the princess. It was entirely *im*possible.

If Lysias put the young princess in the tunnel, and his parents did not get to her, then likely someone awful had. If she had not died, she'd likely met terrible things and *then* died. It was far more plausible that Alexandra was simply from the island, that she'd been caught up in the violence of the coup— perhaps even her parents had been perpetrators in the whole thing. They or she had escaped or been exiled to Athens, and then she'd either been abandoned or orphaned.

A much more plausible story than being a *princess*.

She swept into Diamandis's office without waiting for him. There was an older gentleman standing next to a little table where a variety of small tools where arranged. She smiled at him, putting everything of the past hour behind her. "Good morning."

He was clearly flustered that she'd approached him without the king, but Diamandis soon showed up, Lysias behind him, both looking thunderous. It didn't appear as though they'd physically fought each other though.

So there was that.

"Dr. Nikolaou," Diamandis greeted brusquely. "This is the woman I'd like you to test."

The doctor nodded at her. "Simply have a seat, miss."

So she did. Let the doctor swab her mouth with his little cotton swab and pack it away carefully like it might be gold. "That should be what we need," the doctor said as he began to pack up his materials.

"When will we have the results?" Lysias demanded.

The doctor didn't even look up. "A few days. Friday at the latest."

"I don't need to remind you of how important privacy is in this endeavor, Doctor," Diamandis said coldly.

The doctor looked up at him, and maybe Alexandra was seeing things, or maybe she was overly suspicious. But there was something like hatred in the doctor's eyes. "Of course."

The doctor left without looking at her or Lysias. Lysias had said he was falsifying the results. Did that mean the doctor was under Lysias's influence?

And would Lysias do as he'd promised and search for her real genetic family?

Diamandis turned his attention to Lysias. "You are both dismissed, and you will stay out of the family wing, or I will throw you in a cell. Again." Diamandis did not look at *her*, she noted, so she moved before him.

She studied the angry man and decided to fight all that anger and rage with something else entirely. Because he'd become king at the age of fourteen after his family had been brutally murdered. Maybe like Lysias, maybe like herself, he had not seen gentleness since.

She approached him, took his hands in hers. "I look forward to the answers, Diamandis. It will never be able to answer all our questions, but I hope it will bring us both some clarity. So that you may set some of this anger aside."

He jerked his hands away from her, but she did not let him respond in any other way. She simply turned on a heel and followed the doctor's exit out of the large doors.

Lysias found himself standing shoulder to shoulder with Diamandis, watching Alexandra's graceful exit. Much like upstairs.

She could be the princess.

But it was impossible. It had to be impossible. She found secret doors because she'd been a spy. She had nightmares because, much like him, something terrible had happened to her in her childhood.

But it didn't mean it was the *same* terrible somethings.

The odds were impossible, or so he told himself over and over again. But as the memories forced themselves on him, clearer than they'd been in years, he just kept seeing the princess in Alexandra's brown eyes.

"She's a liar," Diamandis growled. "As are you."

"And yet you keep us here," Lysias replied, trying to find his lazy veneer. Trying to remember what was important. His plans. Falsifying the DNA results.

Are you sure you need to?

"I will prove to my people, and all their whispers, that you are the scheming traitor, just as your parents were. And you will face the wrath not just of me but all of Kalyva."

"Such a shame I am a grown man these days, not so easily conquered instead of an orphaned boy—due to you, I might add. I will not be so easy to sweep aside this time."

"I did not…" But whatever Diamandis had meant to deny, he stopped himself as a young woman appeared at the open office doors. She held a clipboard and curtsied prettily to the king. "Your Majesty, Mr. Kronos is here."

Diamandis nodded at her, then turned his attention to Lysias. "You will not win." He pointed at the door: a clear sign he would not leave until Lysias left first.

Lysias considered a standoff. Simply waiting for Diamandis to bodily remove him, but they'd already tempted their tempers and nearly come to blows.

Only Alexandra's clear lack of interest in their fighting seemed to cure them of their bloodlust.

She really was a wonder. And if he was honest

with himself, he did not want to have to go back to their quarters and face her.

Her questions. Her memories. The feelings that lurked in her eyes.

But he would not be a coward. So he bowed at the king with a sardonic lift of his brow, flashed the assistant a charming smile, then walked back to his and Alexandra's quarters.

He found her standing on the balcony, much as she had been last night. His body hardened at the thought, the desire as intense as it had been, but there was something else. A vulnerability from being in Zandra's room, from the things Alexandra seemed to know...

He would find a way to keep his hands off her. He would keep his physical distance. He could not risk a repeat performance. He had always prized his control, but nothing had ever tested it as Alexandra did.

So he would simply not let himself be tested.

She turned as if she sensed him.

They studied each other across the way for quite some time. Eventually, she came back inside, but she still stood by the balcony door. "Does the doctor work for you?" she asked.

"No, but he was willing to help set the wheels of justice in motion."

Her curiosity morphed into a frown. "What does that mean?"

"People are tired of Diamandis's iron reign. The king has made many errors in seeking to make up for his parents'. He is too hard, too controlling. The people do not love him. He has lost the trust of many."

Her brow furrowed. "You're not planning…"

He might have been offended at what she insinuated, but bloody coups *had* crossed his mind. If he hadn't known so many vulnerable innocent bystanders in the coup he'd survived, he might have used it.

But he only wished to harm Diamandis. Not innocents. "I am not a murderer, Alexandra," he chastised. "Not like Diamandis. I will not have him executed. I will simply have him lose his throne and give Kalyva to the people. His place as king is all that matters to him. Living without it will harm him more than ending his pitiful life."

She began to cross to him, but he could not allow her to get close. It was too much to risk. "I have much to do," he said abruptly. "I will sneak away from the palace to do it. I may not be back until morning this time."

She stared at him for a long moment, almost as if she understood exactly what he was doing. "All right."

"We will attend the ball Friday night, and then Saturday will be the council meeting. Diamandis will be deemed unfit. You will be gone by evening, with your earnings."

"And what will happen to Kalyva?"

Lysias shrugged. "Whatever the people wish."

She showed no response. Just kept looking up at him so that he had to look away or remember shadows. The questions.

"I could go with you tonight," she offered. Not

timidly. Not as if she were afraid he would say no. In the same way she'd always spoken to him. Because there was no timidness in his Al.

"Unnecessary," he said, likely too harshly for the situation.

"I didn't say it had to be necessary." She stood in front of him now. Put her hand on his chest.

He ignored the fire within. Focused on the cold glint of revenge.

"I'm offering my company, Lysias. Not my services."

"No."

She sighed. "Very well. But you could kiss me goodbye." She tilted her face to his, a dangerous knowing in the brown depths of her eyes.

She was smiling, tempting him. Poking at him. But he would not give in. "I will be back in the morning," he said, and turned for the door.

"I know you're afraid, Lysias," she said quietly but firmly. "But I also know you are brave. You tried to save the princess at your own peril. You survived losing everything as a *boy*. Because you survive. Because you are you. You needn't be afraid of me."

He turned back to face her down, because in this he was certain. "But I am not, *asteri mou*. Fear has nothing to do with it."

She said nothing, at first. He made it out the door, but before it closed behind him, he heard her say one thing.

"Yes, it does."

CHAPTER FOURTEEN

LYSIAS WAS TRUE to his word. He did not reappear until morning. Alexandra could admit it was a disappointment. She did not wish for distance, and she thought she'd been very considerate of his feelings by not telling him she loved him.

Of course, she had told him he was afraid. No doubt that was a deep affront to Lysias.

But he acted unchanged in the morning. Perhaps stiffer, more like the man she'd first met, whose only focus was revenge. And he maintained that as he spent the days leading up to the ball, keeping her busy during the day—and staying far away from her at night.

He showed her around the island—or pretended to, as there was always media in tow, snapping their pictures, shouting questions, usually to Lysias, as if she didn't know how to speak at all.

It shouldn't frustrate her. It shouldn't matter, but every day she felt more an imposter and less an avenging angel.

She went to meet with the woman Lysias had hired to make her a dress for the ball and had measurements taken, alterations done. It was a beautiful gown. Ornate and fit for a princess, with golds and blues threaded through that reminded Alexandra of much of the art in the palace. The dramatic cape attached the gown made it stand out—different and fussier than what most other women would be wearing, she had been told.

After her final alteration meeting, Lysias picked her up, and they went to lunch with a young journalist who seemed in awe of them both. Asking Lysias about his meteoric rise and Alexandra about her memory.

Alexandra smiled and played the part, even as a headache drummed behind her eyes. She was growing tired of performing. Of plastering fake smiles on her face while Lysias sat beside her but was clearly a million miles away.

He never looked her in the eye, and it was a loss that made Alexandra question too much. She'd been so sure she could handle this, but the more he withdrew from her, the more she felt the loss like a grief she had never fully known before.

But she smiled at the journalist, didn't need to feign any loving looks at Lysias for the cameras.

Because she did love him, even when that love hurt.

"We used a computer program to age Princess Zandra's royal portrait to how old she would be now," the journalist said, pushing a piece of paper toward them. "Can you believe the results?"

Alexandra looked down at the picture. It looked so much like her reflection, she could only stare, her heart beginning to thunder in her ears. An uneasy jangle of nerves and the hot liquid behind her eyes she'd yet to let spill.

She was very afraid they would. Here and now for all and sundry to see. "You used my picture though?" She looked up at the journalist, desperate for an answer to this that would set her at ease. "I mean, my picture now? That's why it looks so similar?"

The woman shook her head, her eyes alive with excitement. "No, seriously, the computer did all that with just the old portrait. Isn't it amazing what the program can do? It's right on. We're going to run it with the profile on your engagement to Mr. Balaskas." The journalist smiled at Lysias. "I think you'll be very pleased with the results."

Lysias smiled back. "*Efcharistó*, Ms. Karras. I cannot wait to read it. But I must take Alexandra back to the palace. We have many meetings yet today."

Lysias stood, so Alexandra did too, her fake smile plastered as the journalist went on and on and even followed them out to their car. Chattering. Chattering. So that Alexandra's head pounded as her stomach churned.

Because all Alexandra could think about was that picture. It looked *just* like her. Surely, the girl was lying. They'd used her new pictures. It was a fake. A fraud. Maybe Lysias had even paid her to do that. He seemed to be paying everyone to do *something*.

Panic was sitting on her chest, and she did not for the life of her understand why. When Lysias drove by the beach on the way to the palace, she ordered him to stop.

He looked at her skeptically but slowed. "Is something amiss?"

Everything. Everything.

"I need air," she managed to say, throwing herself from the car. She strode down to the water, the flowing skirts tangling around her legs as the tang of sea met her nostrils. She slipped out of her shoes and left them where they laid as she continued toward the water.

She had the strangest impulse to run right into the sea. To swim far away, as far as she could go, and just see what happened. A wave splashed against her toes, cool against the heat of the afternoon, and it reminded her there was nowhere to go.

She wanted to fall to her knees and cry, but she did not. She simply stopped her forward movement and found some comfort in the maternal rocking of the waves. She sucked in a deep breath and calmed herself.

Like she'd done so many times before when she'd narrowly escaped danger in her old life. Her old life that seemed so far away. So behind her, even though it was all she'd known a week ago.

She felt Lysias come stand beside her, but she could not look at him. Not while such emotions warred within her. Her complicated identity, the holes in her memory, her connection to the palace. To *him*.

His hand curled over hers, but she knew this was not for *her*. She could tell in the stiff way he held himself. In the fact he did not murmur her name or call her his star as he so often did.

No, this was for the cameras. She stepped away from his grasp.

"Mind the cameras, Alexandra," he warned coolly.

She wanted to throw a grand tantrum *for the cameras*, but she didn't. It wouldn't get her anything she wanted anyway. But when she spoke, she spoke with clear honesty even if she didn't throw him angry looks. "I don't care about the stupid cameras. I need a moment to breathe. To…be myself. To not have to be someone *else*." She felt as if her lungs had been tied in knots. Why couldn't she breathe?

"You lived as a boy for decades, and suddenly you need to be yourself?" he replied with his usual distant sarcasm.

"Yes. A boy. A nameless, unimportant boy. Not a real-life person." She turned to face him then because she could not argue with the implacable sea. Might as well argue with the implacable man standing next to her. "Not a *princess* who people actually knew. Who's probably dead, and if she is not…"

She might be me.

That picture… It *had* been her. Real or fake, she didn't know, but it rattled her to the bone.

It terrified her to believe it possible, but the signs kept piling up, and she could only deny so much for so long. What if she *was* Zandra? What then?

She was almost too embarrassed to voice that to Lysias. He thought it was impossible, and it should be. It *should* be.

But what if…

She should not ask. She knew, deep in her bones, his response would only hurt her. It wouldn't be what she wanted. And yet there was some tiny sliver of hope that what had come to pass between them might change *something*. "Lysias," she said, taking the hand she'd stepped away from only seconds earlier. She gripped it in some kind of desperation as she looked up at him, tears sliding over her cheeks. "Lysias… what if I am her?"

His expression and voiced hardened. "You're not."

"I didn't ask if I was," she replied, still clutching his hand, though he held himself stiff and closed off. Even as he looked away. Out to sea. "I said *what if?*"

"It would be of no matter," he said, clearly not knowing or caring the words shattered her heart to pieces. He kept his gaze on the waves. "Nothing would change. My plan, my revenge, it remains the same regardless of who you are or ever were."

"Because I am unimportant?" she asked, ragged. A glutton for punishment, apparently.

He looked at her now, and there was *nothing* in

his golden gaze. No heat, no hurt, none of the fear or confusion she'd seen flash there. "You're an important tool, but you are only a tool."

She knew this. Or had known it. She had been naive, apparently. She would forgive herself for that at some point, but for now, she had to set it aside. Survive this. Survive him. "Then I could stay. After your revenge is enacted, I could stay, because I belong here. If I am her."

"It would not be safe for you to stay."

"You mean it would not be safe for *you*. Because I might tell the truth. Because someone might find out *you* were behind the vote of no confidence. But if I'm not here, you can blame it on me."

He did not flinch. No guilt lurked in his eyes. He was blank. Perhaps down to his soul. Perhaps he had no soul left. "There will be no need for anyone to blame. And trust me, Diamandis will know it was me. I will make sure of it. This was never about you, Alexandra."

A stab through the heart, but only fair. Of course it wasn't. Nothing ever had been.

She suddenly felt exhausted. So tired she couldn't hold herself up. "I want to go…" She'd almost said *home*. But she had no home. Not a hovel in Athens, not Lysias's house outside the city, not the palace here.

Lysias felt like home, but he would be gone. He did not view her the same at all. And she had to find some peace there. Because she would not back out now. She'd come this far. She wanted her money.

You want him to change his mind.

Maybe she did. Maybe that made her weak. She would work it out...at some point. But not now. They walked back to the car, and Lysias drove them to the palace. They walked to their rooms, guards trailing after them, everyone silent.

They stepped inside their quarters, and Alexandra did not look at him. She strode for the bedroom and, once inside, turned to face him. He was moving as if he would follow her in, but for the first time, she didn't want to be near him.

"I think I would like to be alone," she said, and closed the door on his face.

Lysias stared at the door, beyond shocked. He did not understand for the life of him what had changed in her. What had altered.

Surely she didn't think she was the princess. It was a ridiculous avenue to go down. He'd been telling himself that for days. On a loop. Because it was, quite simply, *unfathomable.*

And, as he'd told her. That impossibility would change nothing. Nothing could change. His plans were set in stone.

He turned away from the door. No matter what she was thinking or feeling. No matter that she'd cried and that he'd wanted to gather her close and promise her whatever she wished.

No *matter*. Because revenge was in the cards. So he left her. For the rest of the day. Yet again, he did not return to their quarters to sleep. The past few nights, he'd prowled about the island, meeting with whom he needed to meet, catching snatches of sleep in corners and alleys much like he had as an adolescent in Athens.

Tonight, however, he snuck down to the servants' quarters. It was late and mostly quiet, so it was easy to slip into his old rooms. Diamandis had wanted him to stay here, and for some reason that he did not wish to examine, Lysias wanted to prove he could. Even if only to himself.

It was not exactly the same as when he'd been a child, and it was clear no one lived in these rooms. Whether they had stayed unoccupied for years, or Diamandis had some poor family moved out to hurt Lysias, it did not matter.

It was empty and Lysias was here. This room did not scare him. The ghosts of his parents… Now that he was actually in the rooms, he did not feel them here. It was a room like any other.

Perhaps, because no matter how unfairly, they had been in his life less than he had been without them. His memories here were only fond ones. Of good people, good parents, a good childhood before the night that changed everything.

He could picture his mother in the rocking chair doing her mending while his father read on the sofa, his glasses always sliding down his nose. He could picture them working in tandem as they always did.

They had been devoted to one another and, in turn, to him. Something about that realization, that memory, turned uncomfortably over in his chest. Made his heart ache.

So he left the family room and went to the small little room that had been his. No more than a closet, but he'd been happy here. He lay down, right there on the floor, and—thanks to a few days of little rest—fell asleep.

When he woke with a cramp in his neck and his muscles screaming from an uncomfortable night on the floor, he realized that he had not dreamt. Good or bad.

A rarity.

He had no time to consider what that meant because it could mean nothing. Tonight would be the ball.

Tomorrow would be revenge.

Lysias got up. He would need to go back to his quarters and shower and change. And get up there without the guards following him about. But before he could do so, the phone in his pocket buzzed.

"Balaskas," he muttered.

"Mr. Balaskas. I'm sorry to call you directly, but there's a bit of a problem with the DNA test," said the doctor, his voice nervous in Lysias's ear.

"You did not follow my instructions to the letter?" Lysias demanded.

"No, I mean, I followed them exactly, sir," the doctor said, stumbling over his words. "It's just, I cannot do exactly what you want because—"

"I will *destroy* you," Lysias growled, but the doctor was stumbling on, not having the intelligence to shut his traitorous mouth.

"Mr. Balaskas. You don't understand. I created the false test, but then I ran the second test you requested. To discover any genetic matches for the woman. The king *is* a genetic match. Your woman is no imposter. There's an irrefutable sibling percentage match. She *is* the princess. No tampering needed."

Lysias stood with the phone to his ear, but whatever else the doctor said was lost to the buzzing that invaded his mind.

She is the princess.

It could not be. He didn't just pluck a random woman pretending to be a boy out of obscurity only for her to be everything he needed.

Everything indeed.

He managed to thank the doctor, but he hung up on him before he could listen to more of the man's babbling.

He looked around the world of his childhood. Alexandra, his Alexandra, was the princess. Was the little girl he'd saved. She *was* Zandra. All the memories, the resemblances—it was all true.

She would… Would she be happy? Would she revel in the information? He moved forward. She had to know. Immediately. Maybe it would be a difficult discovery for her. It would certainly change…

He stopped halfway to the door. It would change everything.

And it could change nothing.

What had he been thinking? He'd told her just yesterday, even if the impossible were true, it changed nothing.

Now it was so. It was *so*, but it could not alter his plans. The forces were already at work. So she didn't need to know.

He curled his hands into fists.

No one ever need know.

CHAPTER FIFTEEN

ALEXANDRA STUDIED HERSELF in the mirror. She looked every inch the princess as the woman Lysias had hired to prepare her for the ball fluffed her skirts and made last-minute touches to her hair. She tried not to look at the clock again, but it was impossible.

They were meant to make their entrance in less than fifteen minutes. Would Lysias expect her to enter the ball alone? What was he off doing?

Her helper stepped back, examined Alexandra. "Is there anything else you'll be needing, Miss Alexandra?"

"No, thank you." She opened her mouth to ask the woman about Lysias but then decided not to as the woman exited quietly.

Alexandra stood alone in the room dressed up like a princess and felt as alone as she ever had.

Quite the irony for a girl who'd always been alone on the streets. To protect herself and her identity. She had been lonely then, but this was new. Worse. Because it wasn't a generic loneliness. It was loneliness from yearning for a very specific person who'd pulled away from her.

And you let him pull away. You have not told him how you feel. You have only closed doors in his face.

She frowned at the voice in her head, the *truths* if she was only brave enough to look at them. Because she thought Lysias understood the depths of her feelings, but she had not said the words.

Maybe…maybe she could get through to him if she did not allow herself to be distracted or overwhelmed by the situation at hand. If she walked in with her eyes wide open, planning to tell him. *Determined* to tell him, no matter what it cost her.

Except no amount of preparation or clear thinking could have prepared her for Lysias. For what she felt for him. What had grown between them so quickly. She had been prepared to do a job, collect a paycheck.

Not fall in love with a man so afraid of it, he'd avoid her. When she was quite sure he avoided very little.

She needed to decide what to do about it, but maybe it was best to see through Lysias's revenge, *then* worry about what came after.

Like finding out if you're really the princess.

She laughed to herself in the quiet of her room. It was impossible, and she needed to put it out of her head.

A knock sounded at the door. For a moment, her heart tripped over itself, thinking it was Lysias.

But Lysias wouldn't knock. She rolled her eyes at herself and walked over to the door, the heavy cape and dress trailing behind her. She opened it and stepped back at the unexpected arrival. "Um, hello."

King Diamandis moved into the room carefully around her large skirt. A young woman hovered behind him. She was often hovering somewhere around him with a clipboard and a word about his next meeting. Yet Alexandra had never been introduced to the assistant. Apparently he did not plan to introduce them now.

"I thought we should speak before the ball begins. I do not have much time." He looked at the woman with the slim folder. "Knock when it is time," he said to her.

She nodded, then pulled the door closed, leaving Alexandra alone with Diamandis. Nerves and concern fluttered in her chest. But she kept her face carefully arranged in an expression of condescending distrust.

"Whatever we have to discuss should likely wait for Lysias."

"He is not here?"

"He will be," she said with more certainty than she felt.

"Well, I will need to speak to him as well, but perhaps this is better first between the two of us. About the test."

There was something different about the man.

There was still that icy control, a tightly wound posture that spoke of wrought iron determination.

Yet the usual anger did not seem to flame in his eyes, and he stepped forward and gently took her hands in his. Much as she had to him the other day.

"I have heard from the doctor. The DNA match is inarguable. You are indeed Zandra. It's hard for me to fathom how that came to be, but I want to assure you that I am grateful it is. Even if you don't remember me."

She stood, frozen by the words. Words she knew were false. The results were a fake. She wasn't *truly* the princess.

Except you don't know for sure, because Lysias had the results doctored without even finding the truth.

"I suppose it doesn't make much sense to you that I didn't believe. Who else would go around poking throats?" he chuckled, but there was a thickness to his voice that spoke of pure devotion. "My baby sister was the only one I've ever encountered who has done so."

That was why he'd reacted so strangely. The princess had done so to him before. But...

Before she could make sense of it or find words, the door flew open, and Lysias strode in looking furious.

"What are you doing in here?" he demanded of Diamandis.

Diamandis's calm demeanor changed, that flash

of temper back in his eyes. But he didn't tense or drop her hands. "Lysias. The test results have come back."

Lysias eyed Diamandis's hands, then Alexandra's face. She wondered what he saw—what was real reaction and what was an act. She thought she could see through him, but he was nothing but a mask today.

"So, you finally believe me, then?" Lysias said.

The king dropped her hands gently, then fully turned to face Lysias, shoulders back, chin up. He was stiff, formal, but not antagonistic. "I owe you an apology."

Lysias raised an eyebrow. "Naturally."

"Not for disbelieving," the king said, though he was clearly irritated with Lysias's flippancy. "I think I had every right to be suspicious," Diamandis said between gritted teeth. "But I was harder than I needed to be. And more… I don't expect it to matter, to change your opinion of what happened." Diamandis looked back at Alexandra, and she wanted to not believe the kindness she saw lurking in his expression, but surely there was *some* good in this man.

He turned his attention back to Lysias. "I was not the one who gave the order to have your parents executed with the traitors. I was…not myself in the days after the attack. I wrongly relied on my advisors to make the decisions of how to deal with the coup. They have since been dealt with, but it remains a mistake I have regretted for quite some time."

"Perhaps you would have ordered the same if you *had* made the decisions," Lysias replied with absolutely no softening. Even as Alexandra felt herself warm to the man who thought himself her brother.

"Perhaps I would have, you are right," Diamandis agreed. "And I realize this is unforgivable. I do not seek your forgiveness. But I have seen the way you care for her and she for you. So I will grant you my permission for your marriage."

Alexandra's heart twisted. With pain at Diamandis being kind. With guilt over it not being true. And worst of all, longing. That this was all real and true. That she would have a chance to marry Lysias. Maybe even have a family in Diamandis.

But she saw the look on Lysias's face and knew this was not to be.

"I don't recall asking you for permission, Diamandis," Lysias said, wondering if he sounded as casual as he attempted to, or if everything swirling inside of him leaked out through the mask. There was a fury inside of him, and he knew he could not unleash it. His revenge would give him everything he wanted.

But seeing them stand so close… The man who'd once been his best friend, who was *apologizing* and trying to excuse away his parents' murder. The woman…

He'd saved her as a girl. Somehow, some way. He had put her in that tunnel and started some unknown domino of events that had led her here.

Here.

Alive and beautiful. A fierce woman. A fighter, an avenger, and yet there was a softness in her. A great capacity for feeling and passion. There was no one like Alexandra, and on top of all that, she was royalty. The long-lost princess.

"Lysias," Alexandra admonished gently, reaching out to rest her hand over his arm. "Let's try to move forward with some civility."

"It's all right… Zandra," Diamandis said, as if testing out the name.

Because it was *her* name. And Diamandis was *her* brother, and Lysias knew what this would mean to the man he'd once called a friend. So much warred within him, he had to drown it in more of that anger.

Anger that Diamandis would call her that, as if he could sweep away twenty years of pain and suffering. Anger that it was all true, and he did not know how to grapple with it, no matter how many hours he'd tried.

"Her name is Alexandra," he snapped, wishing it were true. "That is the name she goes by. Because, by some miracle, she was spared your inaction, your failures. She might be biologically your sister, but she is *not* Princess Zandra back from the dead simply because you want her to be."

The room plunged into silence, except for the sound of his own ragged breathing. Why couldn't he get control of this? It had to be her fault. She'd done something to him. Unleashed something in him.

He needed to find the tools to put it back. And get the hell out of Kalyva.

"Obviously this is…emotional," Alexandra said softly, her hand still on his arm. "Perhaps we could take some time to individually calm down before we discuss it." Alexandra said. And he *hated* the way she smiled sadly at Diamandis. Who would see it as someone happy but overwhelmed.

But Lysias saw the guilt lurking there. The questions. He could practically see all those wheels turning in her head as she gazed at her brother, not that she knew it. And still…

Still, she wanted to ruin his revenge. He could *see* it.

Diamandis bowed to Alexandra. "I will see you both at the ball, and after tomorrow's council meeting, we will have much time to work through this… Everything. Together."

Alexandra nodded. Lysias did not move. Diamandis exited the room and they both stood as if rooted to the spot.

"We should talk," she said eventually, breaking the spell.

But he could not be alone with her. The truth wanted to escape. And all these damn *feelings*.

"I do not wish to talk," he replied, striding for the door so that her hand fell off his arm. "I wish to make our necessary appearance at the ball. Have you announced princess. I wish to enact the plan in which I am paying you to accomplish. There will be no talking." He opened the door, pointed outside. "Come."

She crossed to him, but she did not walk out the door. She smiled at the guard, then wrenched the door out of Lysias's hands and closed it. "No, Lysias. I'm not going."

CHAPTER SIXTEEN

ALEXANDRA STRUGGLED TO breathe evenly. She felt too much. Hurt too much. She could not go on.

She could not…be part of Diamandis's downfall. Not when he'd seemed truly…humbled. Eager to have some kind of relationship with her. He'd looked at her and called her Zandra, not as if she were a princess.

But as if she were his *sister*.

Her. Who'd never had a family she could remember. Maybe she had memories tied to this place, but…

But you are not the princess.

Maybe, that was the true source of all this pain.

She wanted to be.

She closed her eyes and rested her forehead against the door. She fought against the tears that wanted to fall because she needed to get through to Lysias, and emotional outbursts would not do it.

"You must go to the ball," he said from behind her, his voice like a razor, so sharp, so cutting. "It is what I'm paying you for."

She turned to face him, back against the door, large skirt and cape twisted around her. She curled her fingers into the decadent fabric as if it might grant her some strength.

She couldn't go to the ball now. Now when Diamandis thought...

She'd never expected this to be so hard. What a fool she'd been to think revenge could be simple. Someone always got hurt in the game of payback. She had been okay with that when they had been the distant wealthy figureheads dealing in terrible atrocities.

It was harder to feel righteous when the person was clearly dealing with their own trauma, their own betrayals, their own guilt.

Still, she could not go back in time and undo what had already been done. She could only deal with the events before her.

"Lysias. This no longer feels right."

"It isn't about *right* or how anyone *feels*. It is what's to be done."

She stared at him, wondering if she could get through to him. The pieces of him she'd fallen in love with. Was it love if you couldn't agree with the destruction a person was choosing? Knowing that the destruction wasn't even what he had planned for Diamandis.

It was what enacting his revenge would do to Lysias. He thought his problems, his nightmares, his *pain* would be cured once he hurt Diamandis. He truly believed that.

And she did not know how to combat that belief. She had no great understanding or experience that could prove to him he was wrong. She only had what he was so desperately afraid of. She only had the one thing that would *actually* see him through.

"Lysias, I love you."

There was a beat. A flare in his eyes. But he did not move. He tensed until he seemed to be nothing but a statue. But the statue spoke. So cold. So *lost*. "Love me?" He laughed bitterly. "You know nothing about me. Or love."

"I know you have saved me when you didn't have to. You have protected me. You don't think I've seen the Athenian papers? I know that Vasilis Pangali was finally jailed after ordering that attack on me. And I know you were involved, as I have found so much evidence on that man, and he had never faced any permanent consequence until you saw to it."

"This is irrelevant."

"It isn't. It speaks to who you are and how you care. Underneath the revenge you've sought for so long, you've forgotten why you started on this cursed road to begin with. You are a man who seeks to right wrongs. And that is one of the reasons I love you."

"Alexandra. You will be quiet. You will open that door and we will attend this ball. Tomorrow, I will have my revenge. You will be paid. And then we will part ways. Love has nothing to do with this, and we needn't speak on it any longer."

She wanted to laugh that he thought he could simply order love away or that not speaking on it would change anything. "*I* need to speak on it. I also love you because I understand—along with the luck of the draw—how hard you have worked to become who you are. I know because I did it too. I understand you, Lysias, as few ever will."

"You are full of fairy tales, Al."

And she didn't misunderstand that he'd called her Al for the first time in days on purpose. To create distance. To make her feel like she was only that tool he'd originally sought. But she wasn't Al any longer. *She* had been changed. By what he'd done. By who he was.

"I love you, *Lysias*, because I *know* that beneath the pain you have turned into your armor, there is a man who only wants to belong again. Love again."

"Enough!" he shouted. Loud enough and angrily enough that she did indeed stop.

He stepped forward her, jabbing his finger out as though he meant to poke her in the chest—though he never got close enough to do so.

"You know all these things, but do you know that I had those tests run?" he demanded, a whirlwind of fury and wildness. "The ones you wanted. To try to match you with a family? Did you know that it's true?"

True. The word echoed inside her, a bomb detonating, because he could only mean…

Lysias took her by the shoulders because he needed to touch her. Needed to find his anchor so that he could *fight* her. So he could make her understand that there was nothing about him she could ever love. There was no good in him. Everything in him had died that day twenty years ago, except revenge.

He was made of revenge and revenge only.

"Do you know that it's *all* true?" he said, giving her a small, gentle shake as if it would make the words penetrate. As if he could shake *sense* into her. "You are Princess Zandra, and I have been keeping it from you. And planned to. Forever."

Her eyes were big as she stared up at him. He wanted to see them morph. From all that damn love to confusion, to understanding. To hate.

She should hate him. He wanted her to hate him.

"You…ran the test," she said, but only sounded awed. Only looked up at him as if she'd never doubted him when he was giving her every reason to doubt. To understand. "And you don't see that this was a kindness? Taking care of me. Caring *for* me."

"Are you hearing me? You *are* Zandra. *I knew* and did not tell you."

"When did you find out the results, Lysias?"

He wanted to lie and tell her ages ago, because he knew somehow that she would turn this on him. But he didn't know how to make the lie come out, when he'd never once struggled to lie to get what he wanted. He dropped her shoulders, stepped back. His hands were shaking and this was inexcusable. She was inexcusable.

"When, Lysias?" she demanded.

"This morning," he said. Though it did nothing. Changed nothing. *She* changed nothing. Certainly not twenty years of pain and rage that had driven him. To survive on the streets. To build his empire. To return here triumphant. With the true princess at that.

He refused to acknowledge the little voice in his head that told him she was no different. She too had survived. Had succeeded in her own way. Had somehow found herself back where she belonged.

She could belong to Kalyva. He didn't care. If she wanted to stay, so be it. It mattered not to him. Nothing about her could matter to him.

She could not belong to him.

Alexandra let out a long breath, like a sigh of relief. "Ah, so that's why you stayed away." And she had the gall to *smile*.

"I have been busy."

"Oh, yes, fomenting your peaceful rebellions and what not." She even waved her hand as if this were nothing. As if his whole life's work was *nothing*.

"But really you were avoiding me because you knew you would tell me the truth," she continued. When she didn't know a damned thing. "You have always told me the truth. Except in one thing. Love."

"I do not love, Alexandra. Not anyone." Love was pain. Someone else's power to destroy you. Love was a lie.

"Perhaps this is true. You certainly do not love yourself. Maybe it means you do not have the capacity to love anyone in this moment. But I don't believe that you're incapable or unlovable. I believe all this hate you carry around is just an expression of your love, your grief that was once love."

"That is ludicrous. And it makes no sense." He was desperate for it not to make sense. "If you will not attend the ball with me, then I will attend it without you. You are no longer a necessary pawn, Al. You are simply window dressing now."

There was a flash of hurt in her eyes that landed like a knife to the gut. But he did not go down in pain. He accepted it. Knew it was nothing more than his due.

"How can you hurt him this way?" Alexandra asked, her voice soft. As if she pitied him, and that was the greatest insult in a pile of them.

"He had my parents *killed*."

"You heard him. That wasn't *him*."

"It was him enough. Because I risked my life to save his family, and whether he ordered it or allowed it, he did *nothing* for my parents."

Her shoulders slumped a little, and she did not speak.

"No impassioned rejoinders for that one then?"

"No." She looked at him with that pity—not love,

pity. "I can only beg of you, Lysias. I *beg* of you," she repeated, as if to underscore how important this was. "Do not do this. You don't have to. It doesn't need to be revenge. It could be a life. You could repair your relationship with Diamandis. You could marry me. We could live here on Kalyva, where we belong. We cannot erase twenty years of suffering and survival, but we can *change* that. It can be a happy ending. If you let it."

"There are no happy endings, Alexandra. Because the only endings are bloody coups and death. So I will have my revenge, because anything else would be temporary."

"My love is not temporary," she replied fiercely, with all that warrior's fire. As if it could be true, as if she would *make it so.* As if…

But it was no matter. He did not believe in her love. He would not. "How would you know? You say you know me, but I know *you*, Al. You don't remember your family. You'd never been with a man before me. You have been nothing but alone for all the life you remember. Why would *you* know anything about love?"

If it hurt her, she did not show it. Except perhaps in the way she stood exceptionally still. And had no words to say back to him. But she also did not move—to go to the ball, to get out of his way.

It didn't matter. He could go to the ball without her. He could do *everything* without her.

"If you do not move out of the doorway, I will move you myself."

"You'll regret this course of action, Lysias," she said, her voice vibrating with emotion as she fisted her hand at her own heart, reminding him of all the times she'd done that to him as they'd slept in the same bed. As she'd slept, as she'd dreamt, as she'd cried. "I know you will regret it."

But he regretted this horrible, destructive pain more than he could regret anything else. Why not pile on? Then at least he'd know how to move forward. Pain he could survive. Suffering he could weather. He did not know how to handle any of what she wanted from him. "So be it."

She moved out of the doorway, but as he strode past her, she uttered one last word in a pained whisper. *"Please."*

He stilled, but he could not give in to the way that word cracked through him like shrapnel. "I have given you much, Alexandra. A new life. A reunion with your precious brother. I have restored your crown to you. But you ask too much of me now."

"Perhaps I do," she agreed, surprising him enough so that he turned to look at her over his shoulder.

She looked so beautiful there in that dress. So strong, like the warrior she was. Like the royal she was.

"No matter what you do, Lysias. I will love you. That does not change. I will *mourn* for what you do, but I will still love you."

"Then you're a fool."

She lifted her chin, his Alexandra. "As you said. So be it."

And with that, he strode from the room. He would go to the ball. He would enact his revenge. He would have everything because it was *within his grasp*.

And he no longer needed her to accomplish any of it.

CHAPTER SEVENTEEN

LYSIAS WENT TO the ball. He strode through the palace on the force of his anger, his rage.

His pain.

But he did not go in the main entrance to the ballroom. The guards were busy with the ball itself, so he ducked into the servants' wing and took the narrow hallways toward the ballroom. Everyone was too busy bustling around, getting things accomplished for the ball, to care that he did not belong here. He took a twisting empty hall that would lead him to a little platform above the ballroom. Sometimes performers sang up here to the crowd below. Or had back when he'd been a boy.

Tonight, it gave him a familiar vantage point of the ball. He'd done this as a boy as well. Always hoping to watch Diamandis do something embarrassing so he could make fun of him afterwards.

And perhaps because he'd enjoyed the glitter, the opulence, the spectacle of it all. His parents had been happy in their comfortable, plain lives, but Lysias had always been drawn to the royal production of it all.

He looked down at the sea of flowers and sparkling lights and expensive gowns. The hum of conversation, the plaintive vibration of string instruments.

For twenty years, Lysias had banished every pleasant thought of this place, and he assumed this ball would only bring back bad memories. He'd been a servant. Foolishly friends with a prince. Naively happy in his servitude.

And he had been naive, to a great many things, but underneath all the real-world implications of his position, at twelve, he had been loved. By his parents. People had always been kind to him. He had felt safe here.

And then a group of people—whether they'd had reasons or not—had violently ripped that safety from him. But not just him.

Diamandis and Alexandra as well.

Lysias found the king on the front stage. Diamandis stood as his father once had many years ago. He looked so much like his father, but there was a coldness to him that King Youkilis had never had. Not *ever*.

Diamandis had not had this inside of him back then either. Oh, the Diamandis who Lysias had known had always had a nasty temper. Though they were friends, they'd often gotten into little tussles—often egged on by the boys…the dead boys.

Diamandis had lost much, as Lysias had. As Alexandra had, whether she remembered or not.

Still, he could not let her ridiculous speech soften him to his cause. So Diamandis had lost? This was of no fault of Lysias or his parents. Why shouldn't Diamandis lose *more* for the way he had handled that loss.

At fourteen.

Damn Alexandra. Damn her to hell. He could not alter his plan. He could not give her what she wanted.

If he did…

She would think there was a chance for them when there could never be. She would believe in love. She would think herself safe, and then something would happen to rip it away from both of them.

It was the way of the world. Even his billions could not protect him from tragedy, from loss.

But he could protect her from it. He could protect *her.* It would mean giving up everything…

Lysias looked down at the glittering life he'd once envied and was now a part of, if he wanted to be. He could be in the midst of it. He could be swirling Alexandra around the dance floor if he wanted to.

Except she was a princess. And he was the child of servants.

She did not understand this yet, but it would be made plain to her. And all her grand talk of *love* would evaporate. Once she understood the difference in their stations, she would do just as Diamandis had.

Turn her back on him.

He would not allow it.

And still…the thought of enacting his twenty-year revenge left him feeling sick.

It would be better to wash his hands of this place. Forever. Once and for all. Leave Zandra here so that Diamandis had to always live with the fact that Lysias was the one who'd returned her to him. Lysias would return to his life in Athens. Throw himself into his work once more. Erase all mention and existence of Kalyva, Diamandis and Alexandra from his mind.

Yes, *that* was the answer. Get as far away from this as he could. Forever.

He climbed down from the platform, cut back through the way he'd come, once again fueled by something. Not anger this time.

Fear, Alexandra's voice whispered inside of him.

But she was wrong. *Wrong*. He entered the ballroom and ignored anyone who spoke his name. He did not smile. He made a beeline for the king.

He went right up to Diamandis, didn't bother to acknowledge that the king was speaking with people.

"I need to talk to you. Privately," Lysias said.

Diamandis's eyebrows raised. "Can it *wait*?" the king said through gritted teeth, keeping his smile on the couple he'd been talking to.

"It cannot."

Diamandis sighed, motioned for his assistant. "You'll have to excuse me. Perhaps you can give your information to Miss Floros, and I can be in contact with you soon regarding the matter."

The assistant moved forward with her ever-present clipboard, and Diamandis led Lysias out of the ballroom.

"We need privacy," Lysias said.

"Very well, we may use my office. Is Zandra all right?" he said as they strode through the halls. "She has not arrived yet."

"She is, but you are not."

Diamandis frowned at this but led Lysias into his office, closing the doors behind them. Diamandis stared at him suspiciously but crossed to his desk and leaned a hip on the corner.

"Go on," Diamandis said.

All that ferocious anger and hatred the king had first held toward Lysias was…missing. As if finding out Alexandra was Zandra cured everything.

Could it be that simple? That Zandra was alive, so all the pain and suffering of the past twenty years could be swept away? Forgiven?

But why would life be that simple? That was a childish way of viewing things. That was the way he'd viewed things at twelve. He had survived too long to believe in something as simple as forgiveness. How could he forgive a man who'd been instrumental in his parents' death? How would Diamandis forgive a man who'd stripped him of his crown?

Forgiveness was a childish pipe dream. Nearly as bad as love.

"There will be a vote of no confidence at your council meeting tomorrow," Lysias said, and it was almost as if he floated outside his body. Watching himself ruin everything he'd worked twenty years for. "Everything is in motion, but I can stop it."

"Is that so?" Diamandis replied. He was calm, but Lysias recognized the seething temper underneath.

"It is. And I will stop it. If you meet three demands."

"Demands. So, you've come all this way to blackmail me? Well, that makes more sense than you having heart enough to return Zandra to me."

She is not yours. She is mine.

But that wasn't true, and not only because Alexandra was her own person. "It was meant to be revenge. You can thank your sister for the downgrade to blackmail."

"I hope these asks will be reasonable," Diamandis replied, sounding bored. But his gaze was direct, explorative.

"It won't matter if they are. You will meet them, or you will lose. First, you will have my parents' graves marked. You will absolve them of all wrongdoing in every law, every history book. *Everywhere.*"

"This is not an ask, Lysias. Zandra being alive is proof enough that they were not part of the plot to murder her. I had already begun to set this into motion the moment the doctor called me."

A band around Lysias's heart loosened, and he did not understand this. That a weight he'd carried since then and assumed would always be there would simply…lift. All because he'd asked, and Diamandis had agreed.

And not even because of the blackmail. He'd already started to right the wrongs. Diamandis had been clearing his parents' names as if the truth mattered, as if he could admit a mistake, as if he could make what few amends there were to make.

Impossible.

"Second," Lysias continued, needing to hurry, to finish. So he could leave Kalyva once and for all. Before he had to *feel* anything. "You will take care of and protect Alexandra at all costs."

"She is my sister."

"I want it written into law."

"It already is. She *is* alive, so she *is* the princess. All laws protect her. Ensure her place."

Why was this so easy? Why wasn't Diamandis arguing with him? Why…

It did not matter. It only mattered he finish. He escape.

"And what is your third condition?" Diamandis asked.

"That when she asks where I've gone, you tell her that you uncovered my potential revenge, and you paid me a significant amount of money to undo it all and disappear from Kalyva forever."

Diamandis's brow furrowed. "Why would you wish her to believe such a thing?"

"It is of no matter. These are my requirements.

Either they are done, or you lose your crown tomorrow. And if you go back on any of these promises, I will ensure you lose it in the future. You will never be able to hunt down all who helped me. Revenge is *always* an option."

"But you choose not to use it tomorrow. Because of Zandra," Diamandis said slowly, as if he did not understand what Lysias was doing.

Do you *understand what you're doing?*

What did it matter if he understood, as long as he did it? As long as he escaped.

"Very well," Diamandis said as if he sensed Lysias's urgency at being gone. He reached out a hand. "Consider it done."

Lysias did not shake the king's hand. He turned and left. The palace. Kalyva. And vowed he would never ever return.

Lysias never came back. For a while, Alexandra had considered going to the ball after all. It seemed a shame to waste her fancy dress.

But she was a princess now. Truly the princess. So she would likely have more opportunities to wear it, and she did not feel like smiling at anyone tonight. So she got undressed and allowed herself the luxury of crying herself to sleep.

Because she was safe. Found. Maybe she was heartbroken, but this was... It was not the catastrophe Lysias seemed to think it was. To Alexandra, it was something of a novelty. To care so much for someone they could hurt you… She could only see it as a blessing after twenty years with no one.

So she wept and grieved, and then she slept. In the early hours of morning, she dressed and prepared to find Diamandis so she could warn him of Lysias's revenge. She was still conflicted about the decision since she knew Lysias would see it as yet another betrayal, but she was saving him from himself. And if he gave her the opportunity to explain herself—

No. She wouldn't wait for him to *give* her the opportunity, she would *take* it. Maybe Alexandra, Zandra, whoever she was from this point on, was someone new. But she was also still Al. Still strong and fierce and determined.

Maybe Lysias would be a brick wall *forever*. Then she would spend forever taking it apart brick by brick.

Alexandra opened the door to the hall and was shocked to discover there was no guard. Alexandra could not decide if this was a good development or a terrible one. She crept down the hall, feeling a bit like a burglar.

But when she stepped out of it into the large foyer that offered her different hallways and staircases to different parts of the palace, she saw Diamandis. Sitting on a bench as he looked through his phone, his assistant standing next to him.

When she stepped forward, he looked up, then stood. "Good morning, Zandra," he said, greeting her.

She looked from him to his assistant, looking for

some kind of hint at what this was. "Have you been… waiting for me?"

"I wished to speak with you before my council meeting but did not wish to disturb you."

She took a deep breath to steady herself. "Yes, about the meeting, Diamandis."

He cocked his head, furrowed his brow. "You knew of his plans?" he asked.

"I… *You* know of his plans?"

"Yes, Lysias came to me in a fury last night. Went on about revenge and votes of no confidence, then demanded a large payout to avoid such eventualities. All in the middle of the ball, I might add."

"A payout. I…" Alexandra tried to make sense of this, but she could not. Lysias didn't need money. No doubt Diamandis was not hurt by offering money. "I do not understand."

"I don't either." Diamandis shrugged. As if it didn't matter. As if it was nothing.

It couldn't be nothing. Had she gotten through to him? And if she had, if he'd listened to her about revenge, why would he take money? Why would he not *be* here?

"Zandra," Diamandis said gently, moving forward and after a brief hesitation setting his hands on her shoulders. "I do not believe he intends to return to Kalyva. I think he simply wanted his petty revenge and then to be gone."

"He isn't petty, Diamandis. He is hurting."

Diamandis looked at her with abject pity, but she was still reeling too much to fully absorb any offense.

"I know he has made a big deal in the press about your engagement, but I can do everything in my power to ensure that he is the one held responsible for the breaking of it. You have the full force of the royal—"

"We are still engaged, Diamandis," she said, even knowing it hadn't ever been real in the first place. Even knowing Lysias had no plans to marry her. And still, she could not accept the idea that it was simply…over.

If that made her an object of pity, so be it.

"Zandra—"

"That is *not* my name," she snapped. Then squeezed her eyes shut in regret. "I'm sorry." She reached up and patted his hand on her shoulder. "I do wish… I am so happy to know I am the princess, that I am your sister." She looked up at him. "I want to be Zandra, but…I cannot just ignore the past twenty years. They are a part of me."

And maybe that was what Lysias needed to face. That he could not demarcate time. That his revenge— enacted or not—was never going to erase his twenty years of exile. He could not win and forget.

He had to accept. And heal.

"I will try to be more cognizant of that," Diamandis said, a little stiffly but clearly still trying to be kind. Warm.

She smiled at him. She knew he'd been a strange

kind of victim here. The weight of remembering could not be easy. "Do you think we'll ever know how I escaped?"

"I have spent twenty years trying to find an answer that wasn't your death, but I've found nothing. We will keep looking though."

"No. No, I think maybe it is best not to know. Best to just be grateful for what we have. What we *can* have." In a future, without Lysias. "Though to be honest, I haven't the first clue what the next step in my life is."

"You needn't worry about it. You're home."

But that didn't feel right. Of course, without Lysias, very little *felt* right. She still could not understand why he would have taken *money* and not his revenge. Why he'd listened to her, but then not returned to her.

"He made Diamandis promise not to tell you the truth," the assistant blurted from where she hovered just out of sight.

The king whirled on the woman even as Alexandra tried to make sense of her words.

"What are you saying?" Diamandis hissed.

"He made *you* promise not to tell," the assistant said, lifting her chin at the king. "Not me."

"He didn't know you were listening and neither did I."

She shrugged, her gaze settling on Alexandra. "I was right outside the door. He left so quickly and angrily he nearly crushed me with it, so he didn't see me. Zandra, Your Highness, Alexandra, he was *not* paid. He did not want a payment. He wanted—"

"Miss Floros," Diamandis snapped, taking her by the arm and beginning to pull her toward the exit. "You will cease—"

"First, clearing his parents' name," she continued, even as Diamandis pulled her away. She simply turned her head to keep facing Alexandra and spoke louder. "Protecting you—"

"Katerina!" The king almost had her to a door that led somewhere Alexandra had never been.

Still, the brave woman shouted over Diamandis's attempts to silence her. "And not telling you."

He slammed the door on her. Then stood, back to Alexandra, as the words landed. Nonsensical words, of course.

"Diamandis, I don't understand. Is it true?"

Diamandis sighed heavily as he turned to face her. "I had to meet all three demands to keep him from enacting his little revenge, Zandra. If you know, then I have not kept up my end of the bargain."

She shook her head. There would be no revenge. Not now. Not ever. "I shall keep it for you." Because Lysias had changed course, yes, but more than that, he'd ensured her protection and wanted that kept from her?

Perhaps it was warped, but she knew him. She understood him. It meant he loved her. If he didn't, he wouldn't be afraid. If he didn't, he wouldn't have changed his twenty-year revenge plot. Only love could have done that.

Only love. The thing he was so afraid of. Afraid enough that the powerful, determined, proud Lysias had run away. Like the hurting boy he was on the inside.

She supposed she could sit around and wait for him to realize it. He would eventually. He was too... enduring not to.

But she didn't want to wait around. She too had endured, and she wanted more. And to not waste a moment of that more.

"I must go to Athens, Diamandis. But I will be back. Mark my words, we'll both be back."

"You will be welcome. Him?"

"He will also be welcome," she replied firmly. "Because I love him, and I am the princess." Still such an odd thing to say, to be real. But she wanted to hold on to it for dear life. It and Lysias. "For all his faults, he is a good man at heart. I think you must be able to understand where his struggles come from. How hard it is to believe in good when it was so cruelly stripped from you so young."

Diamandis grunted. "You need only ask Michelis. His office is in the front hall. He has been instructed to take you wherever you want," he grumbled.

Alexandra turned to move, but Diamandis stood in her way. "I know we do not truly know each other, but I am your brother. And the king of Kalyva. No matter what happens, know you always have a place here. And I will always be a safe place to land." He looked so kind in the moment, so vulnerable, Alexandra followed her impulse.

She wrapped her arms around him and held on to him tightly, blinking back the tears. "Thank you. I may never remember those first four years…" She pulled back and looked up at him. "But we have whatever years ahead of us to make up for the ones we lost."

Because she believed in possibilities. In joys and futures and in love.

Now she had to track down her fearsome fiancé and convince him that he could too.

CHAPTER EIGHTEEN

Lysias stared down at Athens from his office window. He was in a foul temper and had instructed his staff that no one bother him. They had listened.

He couldn't seem to concentrate on work. His mind was still back in Kalyva. In the palace. With Alexandra.

Princess Zandra.

Surrounded by all he'd amassed—his position, his money—it was hard to hold on to the idea he was somehow not worthy of someone with her title. It was hard not to acknowledge that the way he felt inferior was born of a system he'd understood only from the eyes of a boy.

Now he was a man. And what he was not worthy of was *her*. Her determination. Her love. Her courage.

He scowled. How had she come to mean so much? How had she crawled into his life and turned it inside out? It had only been a day since the ball, and still he *grieved* that she was not here. That he could not walk down the hall and see her. Not catch a glimpse of her or sleep next to her in his bed.

His life had always felt busy before. Work had filled his days, and revenge had filled everything else. He'd thought that was something.

But Alexandra had shown him it was nothing. She had even ruined his revenge for him. He had not taken Diamandis down a peg, but clearing his parents' name had eased some of the dark guilt that had twisted him up. Some of the injured rage that had kept him going for so long.

He still missed them. Still loved them. Still grieved everything that happened to them and him in the tragedy. But the blinding anger had ceded. All from one simple action by a man he'd been hating as a symbol for twenty years.

Alexandra had been right. His revenge would not have given him that satisfaction. It would only have driven the hate deeper.

So, he had absolutely nothing now. Except his wealth. And his desperate need for a woman he'd left behind.

But he was Lysias Balaskas. He did not *do without* when he could accomplish and obtain everything he wanted. Unfortunately, she was no simple want.

How could he go back to her, knowing what he stood to lose? How could he risk every wall that he'd built, that had allowed him to become Lysias Balaskas, billionaire, success? She threatened everything.

Everything…that she had turned into nothing. How could he live without her?

There was some commotion behind his door, then it swung open, and he heard someone arguing.

"Never mind," a female voice said quite firmly. "I'm sure he will see his fiancée regardless."

That voice. And then she glided into his office as if she belonged there, followed by his stuttering assistant.

"I'm sorry, sir," Marcus said, stumbling.

"Never mind," Lysias muttered, never taking his eyes from Alexandra. "You may leave us."

She was here. He nearly went to her. Without thought. Without hesitation. He wanted her in his arms. He wanted his mouth on hers. He wanted to hear her voice. He'd thought the payoff, the disappearance would insult her enough that she would realize she did not love him, need him.

But here she was.

"Well, what do you have to say for yourself?" she demanded. She was wearing all black, like some kind of avenging ninja. Her eyes were fierce, her voice fiercer.

And he had no words.

"Diamandis's assistant heard your little…whatever you thought you were doing," she continued, prowling over to the wall of windows and peering down at Athens below. Then she turned to him, cut him in half with that dark brown gaze. "You didn't enact your revenge. You asked for very little in return."

"I asked for everything I required, and even that he could not give me if you know about it," he said, but his voice was rough, and his hands itched to grab her. Hold on to her. Bury himself in the scent of her.

"What about what *I* could give you, Lysias?"

"Your love?" he said, trying to sound disgusted, uninterested. Even as it thundered within him. The only answer to all this nothing was her *love*.

"Yes. My love. My forever. Belonging. A home. A family." Her mouth began to curve, which made no earthly sense. "I know you love me."

He wondered when he'd fully accepted the simple truth of that. It had been gradual, not sudden. In retrospect, the more he'd felt out of control in Kalyva, the more focused on revenge, the more he'd been trying to avoid the simple fact.

The unavoidable fact. A truth of life even he could not bend.

Yes, he loved her.

She closed the distance between them, put her small hand over his heart, where the ring he'd given her glittered in the light. "You think love is pain, and you are not wrong, but this is why you surround yourself with it. So when loss inevitably strikes, you lean into the love you still have. The love that can grow. I know you did not mean to, but you have opened a new world for me. You have given me my family back. More love than I dreamed—and I want more of it, Lysias. Not less."

More not less.

"You can run away from me like a boy, but you are not one anymore. You are a grown man, so this is only cowardice. And I will not be afraid. I will chase you down. I will follow you to the ends of the earth to prove my love to you."

"That sounds like stalking, Alexandra."

But her smile only widened. "Then convince me, Lysias, somehow, someway. That you do not love me. I will leave you alone forever if you do."

He lifted his hand to cover hers and he watched her stiffen. As if she were bracing herself for him removing it. As if she weren't as sure as she acted.

It struck him then, that this truly was an act of courage. She had doubts, but she loved him enough, believed in him enough, to set them aside. To put her heart on the line. To chase him down and insist he face the worst parts of himself.

She had asked him to spare Diamandis, and he had. Now she only asked for his heart, and was that really such a terrible thing to give?

So he curled his hand around hers. "Anything could take you from me. I thought it would best to be the one who did it. So I could control it. I can control everything, except the whims of fate."

"Lysias—"

"Allow me to finish, Alexandra. Zandra. So much was taken from me, I decided to take from everyone else. But I wish not to take from you. Only give. For twenty years, I locked old, violent memories away. But also the good ones. Being back at the palace reminded me. Of warmth. Of love. The deep and true kind my parents had for one another and me. And the kind I have for you."

Her expression remained calm, but she sucked in a sharp breath.

"I love you, Al, Alexandra, Zandra, Princess. Whatever name you choose. If you take my last name, I will call you whatever you wish."

She swallowed before she spoke, tears glistening in his eyes. "We haven't even discussed that you saved my life not once but twice."

"Ah, *asteri mou*, but you have saved my heart." He pressed a kiss to her forehead. "So I must thank you."

"You should probably also ask me nicely to be your wife. And smile prettily while you do it."

"No, I will not ask nicely." At her scowl, he bent down onto his knees. "I will beg you, my love."

Her smile bloomed.

"Be my wife. Through all the wonderful things I will ensure life gives us, and through all that life will no doubt take from us. I promise, I will not run away from you ever again. You are my star, my heart, my princess."

The tears that shone in her eyes fell to her cheeks, and she knelt too—so they were knee to knee, hands clutching each other. "I will be all those things, Lysias. And more we cannot imagine yet. But what the future holds does not matter. As long as we are together."

"Forever, *asteri mou*. Forever." And he sealed this promise with a kiss.

EPILOGUE

Three months later

"WE CANNOT SIMPLY move up a royal wedding, Lysias," Diamandis said from behind his desk.

Alexandra sat with Lysias on the settee across from the desk. Lysias held her hand in his. He looked over at her, gave her his mischievous smile. Before straightening and saying to Diamandis very seriously, "The original date poses a problem."

"Do you know everything that would have to be changed? Altered?" Diamandis asked. They'd had a few rows over the past few months. Neither Alexandra nor Lysias were very good at following royal decrees blindly.

But they always found a compromise. They always made up. They were a family. A growing family.

"I realize this is unfortunate and annoying," Alexandra said, matching his officious tone. "But as I might be in labor, it seems irresponsible to go on as planned." She smoothed her hand over her still mostly flat belly. It amazed her that a child grew inside there. They'd kept it to themselves at first, wanting to bask in the glow of it all. But as royal wedding plans ramped up, it seemed imperative to bring Diamandis in on the news.

"You might be…" Diamandis stopped, blanched. "Zandra."

"The doctor confirmed a due date of the same day as the current wedding. Now, of course, we can roll the dice. I have heard babies don't really care about your plans, but she could—"

"She…?" Diamandis said, almost on a whisper. As if he'd never heard of such a thing before.

"Yes, you will have a niece in about six months' time. Which is why I'd like to move the wedding. Now, Lysias and I are already married—"

"Do not remind me of your unsanctioned, irresponsible *Greek* wedding. It does not signify here in Kalyva," Diamandis grumbled.

"Be that as it may, you may choose how you wish to reschedule. Before or after the baby. But it will need to be rescheduled."

Diamandis closed his eyes, breathed in and out slowly. "You couldn't have done this when I had an assistant worth a damn?"

"I do miss Katerina. You never did tell me what you did to run her off."

Diamandis scowled darkly. "We will move the date up if it can be managed. I will let you know.

Now, I have much work to do. Thanks to you two." He waved a hand at them, his attempt at dismissal.

But Alexandra was not so easily dislodged. "We've chosen a name."

"The royal tradition is—"

"Yes, Diamandis. I know. Lysias told me. But it doesn't feel right for me to use our mother's name when I don't remember her, and you may have a daughter someday to use the name on."

"I do not plan to marry. Or have children. This is happy news indeed, as your child will now be considered the heir, and I will be under no pressure to provide one." He said it darkly, and Alexandra felt sympathy for him.

She also looked up at the portrait that hung in his office. Of their parents. She did not remember them, not really, and still she said a little prayer to them.

Give him love, as I have been given.

"We will be happy to use it as a middle name," Lysias said, playing peacemaker, as he sometimes did. Which was rare, but it always amused Alexandra. "But we have decided. We will name our daughter after *my* mother."

Diamandis sighed, clearly incapable of arguing with *that*. "Very well." He pressed a finger to his temple. "You two might be more trouble than you're worth. I hope you know this."

Lysias looked over at her and grinned. "Ah, Diamandis, have you not learned? Love is always worth all the trouble."

Princess Zandra Balaskas grinned right back. "Always," she agreed.

* * * * *

If you fell in love with
Hired for His Royal Revenge,
then look out for the next installment in the
Secrets of the Kalyva Crown duet.

In the meantime, why not check out
Lorraine Hall's debut for Harlequin Presents?
The Prince's Royal Wedding Demand

Available now!

#4105 THE BABY BEHIND THEIR MARRIAGE MERGER
Cape Town Tycoons
by Joss Wood

After one wild weekend with tycoon Jude, VP Addison must confess a most unprofessional secret...she's pregnant! But Jude has a shocking confession of his own: to inherit his business, he *must* legitimize his heir—by making Addi his bride!

#4106 KIDNAPPED FOR THE ACOSTA HEIR
The Acostas!
by Susan Stephens

One unforgettable night with Alejandro leaves Sienna carrying a nine-month secret! But before she has the chance to confess, he discovers the truth and steals her away on his superyacht. Now, Sienna is about to realize how intent Alejandro is on claiming his child...

#4107 ITALIAN NIGHTS TO CLAIM THE VIRGIN
by Sharon Kendrick

Billionaire Alessio can think of nothing worse than attending another fraught family event alone. So, upon finding Nicola moonlighting as a waitress to make ends meet, they strike a bargain. He'll pay the innocent to accompany him to Italy...as his girlfriend!

#4108 WHAT HER SICILIAN HUSBAND DESIRES
by Caitlin Crews

Innocent Chloe married magnate Lao for protection after her father's death. They've lived separate lives since. So, when she's summoned to his breathtaking Sicilian castello, she expects him to demand a divorce. But her husband demands the opposite—an heir!

HPCNMRA0423

#4109 AWAKENED BY HER ULTRA-RICH ENEMY
by Marcella Bell

Convinced that Bjorn, like all wealthy men, is up to no good, photojournalist Lyla sets out to prove it. But when her investigation leads to an accidental injury, she's stranded under her enemy's exhilarating gaze...

#4110 DESERT KING'S FORBIDDEN TEMPTATION
The Long-Lost Cortéz Brothers
by Clare Connelly

To secure his throne, Sheikh Tariq is marrying a princess. It's all very simple until his intended bride's friend and advisor, Eloise, is sent to negotiate the union. And Tariq suddenly finds his unwavering devotion to duty tested...

#4111 CINDERELLA AND THE OUTBACK BILLIONAIRE
Billionaires of the Outback
by Kelly Hunter

When his helicopter crashes, a captivating stranger keeps Reid alive. Under the cover of darkness, a desperate intimacy is kindled. So, when Reid is rescued and his Cinderella savior disappears, he won't rest until he finds her!

#4112 RIVALS AT THE ROYAL ALTAR
by Julieanne Howells

When the off-limits chemistry that Prince Sebastien and Queen Agnesse have long ignored explodes...the consequences are legally binding! They have faced heartbreak apart. But if they can finally believe that love exists...it could help them face their biggest trial *together*.

YOU CAN FIND MORE INFORMATION ON UPCOMING HARLEQUIN TITLES, FREE EXCERPTS AND MORE AT HARLEQUIN.COM.

HPCNMRB0423

Get 4 FREE REWARDS!

We'll send you 2 FREE Books plus 2 FREE Mystery Gifts.

FREE Value Over **$20**

Both the **Harlequin® Desire** and **Harlequin Presents®** series feature compelling novels filled with passion, sensuality and intriguing scandals.

YES! Please send me 2 FREE novels from the Harlequin Desire or Harlequin Presents series and my 2 FREE gifts (gifts are worth about $10 retail). After receiving them, if I don't wish to receive any more books, I can return the shipping statement marked "cancel." If I don't cancel, I will receive 6 brand-new Harlequin Presents Larger-Print books every month and be billed just $6.30 each in the U.S. or $6.49 each in Canada, a savings of at least 10% off the cover price, or 6 Harlequin Desire books every month and be billed just $5.05 each in the U.S. or $5.74 each in Canada, a savings of at least 12% off the cover price. It's quite a bargain! Shipping and handling is just 50¢ per book in the U.S. and $1.25 per book in Canada.* I understand that accepting the 2 free books and gifts places me under no obligation to buy anything. I can always return a shipment and cancel at any time by calling the number below. The free books and gifts are mine to keep no matter what I decide.

Choose one: ☐ **Harlequin Desire**
(225/326 HDN GRJ7)

☐ **Harlequin Presents Larger-Print**
(176/376 HDN GRJ7)

Name (please print)

Address   Apt. #

City   State/Province   Zip/Postal Code

Email: Please check this box ☐ if you would like to receive newsletters and promotional emails from Harlequin Enterprises ULC and its affiliates. You can unsubscribe anytime.

Mail to the Harlequin Reader Service:
IN U.S.A.: P.O. Box 1341, Buffalo, NY 14240-8531
IN CANADA: P.O. Box 603, Fort Erie, Ontario L2A 5X3

Want to try 2 free books from another series! Call 1-800-873-8635 or visit www.ReaderService.com.

---

*Terms and prices subject to change without notice. Prices do not include sales taxes, which will be charged (if applicable) based on your state or country of residence. Canadian residents will be charged applicable taxes. Offer not valid in Quebec. This offer is limited to one order per household. Books received may not be as shown. Not valid for current subscribers to the Harlequin Presents or Harlequin Desire series. All orders subject to approval. Credit or debit balances in a customer's account(s) may be offset by any other outstanding balance owed by or to the customer. Please allow 4 to 6 weeks for delivery. Offer available while quantities last.

Your Privacy—Your information is being collected by Harlequin Enterprises ULC, operating as Harlequin Reader Service. For a complete summary of the information we collect, how we use this information and to whom it is disclosed, please visit our privacy notice located at corporate.harlequin.com/privacy-notice. From time to time we may also exchange your personal information with reputable third parties. If you wish to opt out of this sharing of your personal information, please visit readerservice.com/consumerschoice or call 1-800-873-8635. **Notice to California Residents**—Under California law, you have specific rights to control and access your data. For more information on these rights and how to exercise them, visit corporate.harlequin.com/california-privacy.

HDHP22R3

HARLEQUIN
PLUS

Try the best multimedia subscription service for romance readers like you!

Read, Watch and Play.

Experience the easiest way to get the romance content you crave.

Start your **FREE TRIAL** at
www.harlequinplus.com/freetrial.